P9-CEU-812

THE ROMANCE OF PAULA VAUGHAN

LEISURE ARTS, INC.
Little Rock, Arkansas

Paula Vaughan is a warm and gracious lady who still surrounds herself with many of the wonderful things she remembers from her Mississippi childhood. Her west Tennessee home has a rambling front porch adorned with bright potted flowers — the perfect spot for quiet conversation. Inside, her beautiful quilts are displayed everywhere imaginable, and her kitchen is a cozy haven, featuring a fireplace and a big trestle table.

It's in her airy second-story studio that Paula spins her magic with colorful quilts, wonderful antiques, and her precious memories. When she isn't working there, she may be found combing local antique shops or traveling with her husband in the Great Smoky Mountains, in search of more delightful treasures from yesteryear.

Gentle country images captured in soft pastel watercolors are at the heart of America's love affair with Paula Vaughan. Recreating a bygone era, Paula's paintings seem to express our longing for the simpler times of the past.

Yet there's also a marvelous quality of immediacy in Paula's pictures that fascinates her audiences. Each vignette suggests that a woman from yesteryear has just stepped away and will be returning soon to take up her sewing again or to relax in a rocking chair or porch swing. The tranquility of these sentimental still lifes has endeared Paula's work to many people — especially needlewomen.

For Paula, her art is a mingling of fond childhood memories and delightful antiques from an earlier era. The cozy porches in her paintings reflect the contentment she knew as a child in rural Mississippi, where she spent lazy summer evenings with her grandparents, telling stories or listening to the Grand Ole Opry. It's the love for sewing that her mother and grandmothers passed on that inspires Paula to include the vintage clothing and sewing accessories in many of her pieces. And the patchwork quilts gracing her work speak of the resourceful country women she so admires — women who used their colorful patchwork projects to express themselves artistically.

It was that same sort of yearning for creative expression that prompted Paula to paint her first pictures, using her toddler's high chair as an easel. Before long, her country upbringing spilled over onto her canvases, and once she found that she could capture her beloved treasures best in watercolors, Paula's personal style emerged.

A self-effacing woman, Paula never intended to sell her work. It was only reluctantly that she agreed to display a few of her paintings at an art gallery that had framed some of her pictures. To her surprise, the paintings sold so well that she had to publish prints to keep up with the demand.

Leisure Arts editors discovered Paula's wonderful watercolors in 1985. Convinced that they would translate beautifully into cross stitch, we embarked upon an exciting venture with her that has proven to be both rich and rewarding. Paula's leaflets are among our most well received ones. Over the past eight years, we have translated more than 50 of her delightful scenes to cross stitch and have also published two of her prints.

From the very beginning, Paula's works have been popular with needlewomen. For many, an exciting milestone in their needlework experience has been completing their first Paula Vaughan piece. Because of the intricacy and size, these projects are truly labors of love — destined to become cherished heirlooms.

This special book is a natural extension of our association with Paula. It was inspired by the love that women everywhere have for her art and the old-fashioned quilts, bouquets, and antiques that she immortalizes. The book is divided into six sections, each featuring a nostalgic watercolor scene adapted to cross stitch. In addition to each lovely stitched piece, we have given you a coordinating collection of craft projects patterned after many of the wonderful things portrayed in the picture. You'll find instructions for creating heirloom-quality quilts, linens, and clothing, as well as all kinds of decorative items for your house. It is our hope that you will receive great satisfaction as you create these wonderful treasures and bring the romance of Paula Vaughan into your heart and home!

EDITORIAL STAFF

Editor: Anne Van Wagner Childs
Executive Director: Sandra Graham Case
Creative Art Director: Gloria Bearden
Executive Editor: Susan Frantz Wiles

PRODUCTION
TECHNICAL
Managing Editor: Sherry Taylor O'Connor
Senior Technical Writer: Kathy Rose Bradley
Technical Writers: Chanda English Adams,
   Ann Brawner Turner, Candice Treat Murphy,
   Nancy L. Taylor, and Dawn Kelliher Guthrie

DESIGN
Design Director: Patricia Wallenfang Sowers
Senior Designer: Diana Heien Suttle
Designers: Mary Lillian Hill and Rebecca Sunwall Werle
Craft Assistant: Kathy Womack Jones

EDITORIAL
Associate Editor: Dorothy Latimer Johnson
Senior Editorial Writer: Linda L. Trimble
Editorial Assistant: Laurie R. Burleson
Advertising and Direct Mail Copywriters:
   Steven M. Cooper and Marla Shivers

ART
Production Art Director: Melinda Stout
Senior Production Artist: Michael Spigner
Art Production Assistants: Leslie Loring Krebs,
   Ashley Cole, Deborah Taylor Choate, and
   Diane Ghegan
Typesetters: Cindy Lumpkin and Stephanie Cordero
Advertising and Direct Mail Artist: Linda Lovette

BUSINESS STAFF

Publisher: Steve Patterson
Controller: Tom Siebenmorgen
Retail Sales Director: Richard Tignor
Retail Marketing Director: Pam Stebbins
Retail Customer Services Director: Margaret Sweetin
Marketing Manager: Russ Barnett

Executive Director of Marketing and Circulation:
   Guy A. Crossley
Fulfillment Manager: Byron L. Taylor
Print Production: Nancy Reddick Lister and
   Laura Lockhart

MEMORIES IN THE MAKING SERIES

Copyright© 1993 by Leisure Arts, 5701 Ranch Drive, Little Rock, Arkansas 72212. All rights reserved. No part of this book may be reproduced in any form or by any means without the prior written permission of the publisher, except for brief quotations in reviews appearing in magazines or newspapers. We have made every effort to ensure that these instructions are accurate and complete. We cannot, however, be responsible for human error, typographical mistakes, or variations in individual work. Printed in the United States of America. First Printing.

International Standard Book Number 0-942237-19-6

TABLE OF CONTENTS

TABLE OF CONTENTS

Stolen Moment

Enticing us to step back to a simpler time, this tranquil scene captures the imagination. The relaxed mood makes it easy to envision a woman of yesteryear setting aside her everyday tasks and stealing away to gather wildflowers on a warm summer day. We can almost share such a moment with her by indulging in pastimes of our own that she might have enjoyed — perhaps picnicking in a meadow, strolling alongside a quiet brook, or writing a letter to a dear friend. As we savor the dappled summer sunlight, daydreams of the past are sure to enhance our stolen moment.

Chart, page 16

Summery Straw Hat, page 21

A quiet moment beside a gentle stream refreshes the soul. Providing shade from the sun, a simple straw hat takes on a nostalgic air when adorned with ribbons and flowers. It's so pretty that you'll want to leave it out for all to see — when you're not wearing it, that is!

Feminine bits of ribbon and lace turn a plain white tuxedo shirt and canvas shoes into matching accessories. Reminiscent of the lovely arrangements portrayed in many of Paula's paintings, a basket of silk wildflowers offers an enduring touch of summer.

Wildflower Wearables, page 21
Wildflower Basket, page 23

A warm, sunny day beckons us out of doors for an impromptu picnic. Our fabric-lined picnic basket is dressed up with a plaque decoupaged with fabric cutouts. A picnic cloth with coordinating napkins completes the set. A beautiful crocheted afghan inspired by the Grandmother's Flower Garden quilt — one of Paula's favorite patterns — adds to the pleasure of lounging with a romantic book and a refreshing drink.

Picnic Set, page 20

Flower Garden Afghan, page 24

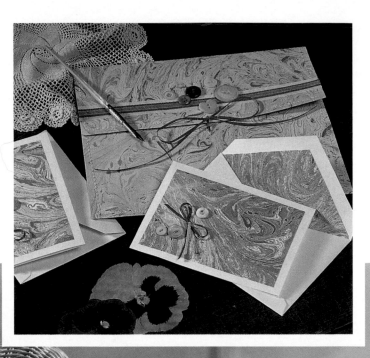

*L*ovingly gathered and pressed, a bouquet of wildflowers is a sentimental keepsake of a special afternoon. When we find ourselves inclined to share our innermost thoughts with a friend, elegant stationery adds joy to the experience. Reflecting a popular Victorian technique, our marbleized paper features colors inspired by the pressed bouquet.

Battenberg lace, ribbons, and other accents from days gone by bring the romance of yesteryear to a white knit cardigan.

Marbleized Stationery, page 25
Pressed Flower Picture, page 23

Battenberg Lace Cardigan, page 22

STOLEN MOMENT (Shown on page 9)

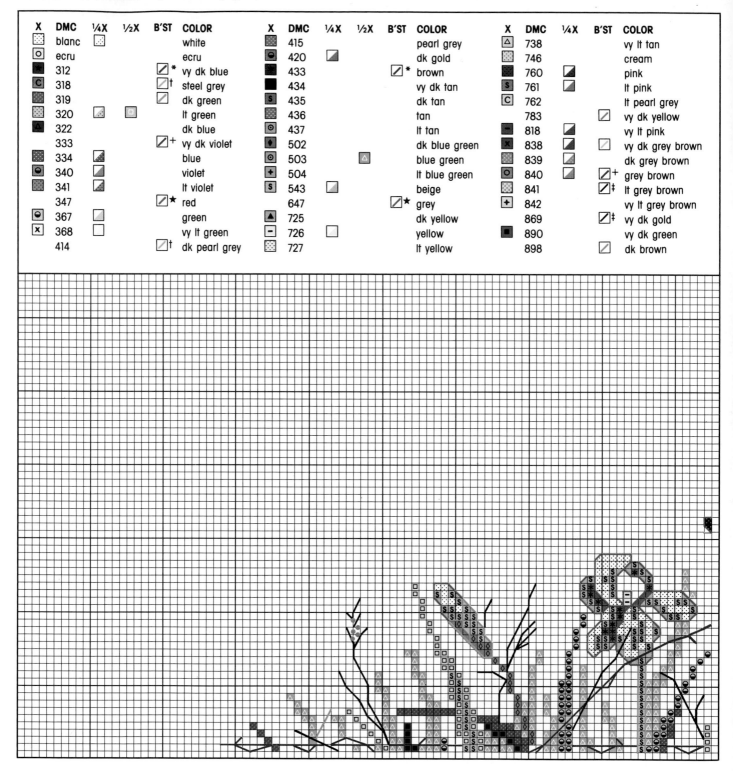

X	DMC	1/4X	1/2X	B'ST	COLOR	X	DMC	1/4X	1/2X	B'ST	COLOR	X	DMC	1/4X	B'ST	COLOR
	blanc				white		415				pearl grey		738			vy lt tan
	ecru				ecru		420	✓			dk gold		746			cream
	312			✓ *	vy dk blue		433			✓ *	brown		760	✓		pink
	318			✓ †	steel grey		434				vy dk tan		761	✓		lt pink
	319			✓	dk green		435				dk tan		762			lt pearl grey
	320	✓			lt green		436				tan		783	✓		vy dk yellow
	322				dk blue		437				lt tan		818		✓	vy lt pink
	333			✓ +	vy dk violet		502				dk blue green		838		✓	vy dk grey brown
	334	✓			blue		503		✓		blue green		839		✓	dk grey brown
	340	✓			violet		504				lt blue green		840		✓ +	grey brown
	341	✓			lt violet		543	✓			beige		841		✓ ‡	lt grey brown
	347			✓ ★	red		647			✓ ★	grey		842			vy lt grey brown
	367	✓			green		725				dk yellow		869		✓ ‡	vy dk gold
	368	✓			vy lt green		726	✓			yellow		890			vy dk green
	414			✓ †	dk pearl grey		727				lt yellow		898		✓	dk brown

X	DMC	¼X	½X	B'ST	COLOR
	3011				olive
	3045				gold
C	3046				lt gold
☆	3047				vy lt gold
*	3072				vy lt grey
	3078				vy lt yellow
-	3325				vy lt blue
◊	3362				dk yellow green
S	3363				yellow green
	3364				lt yellow green
	3685				burgundy
*	3687				mauve
◊	3688				lt mauve
	3712			†	dk pink
	3746				dk violet

X	DMC	¼X	½X	B'ST	COLOR
	3747				vy lt violet
	3755				lt blue
	869	French Knot			vy dk gold
	Pink area indicates last row of previous section of design.				

* Brown for barbed wire. Vy dk blue for all other.

† Steel grey for pins and needle. Dk pearl grey for white basket. Dk pink for roses on hat.

\+ Vy dk violet for bow and fabric in white basket. Grey brown for all other.

★ Grey for irises. Red for all other.

‡ Lt grey brown for quilt blocks. Vy dk gold for all other.

STOLEN MOMENT (154w x 150h)			
14 count	11"	x	10¾"
16 count	9⅝"	x	9⅜"
18 count	8⅝"	x	8⅜"
22 count	7"	x	6⅞"

Stolen Moment (154w x 150h) was stitched over 2 fabric threads on a 21" square of Cream Belfast Linen (32 ct). Two strands of floss were used for Cross Stitch and 1 for all other stitches. The design was custom framed.

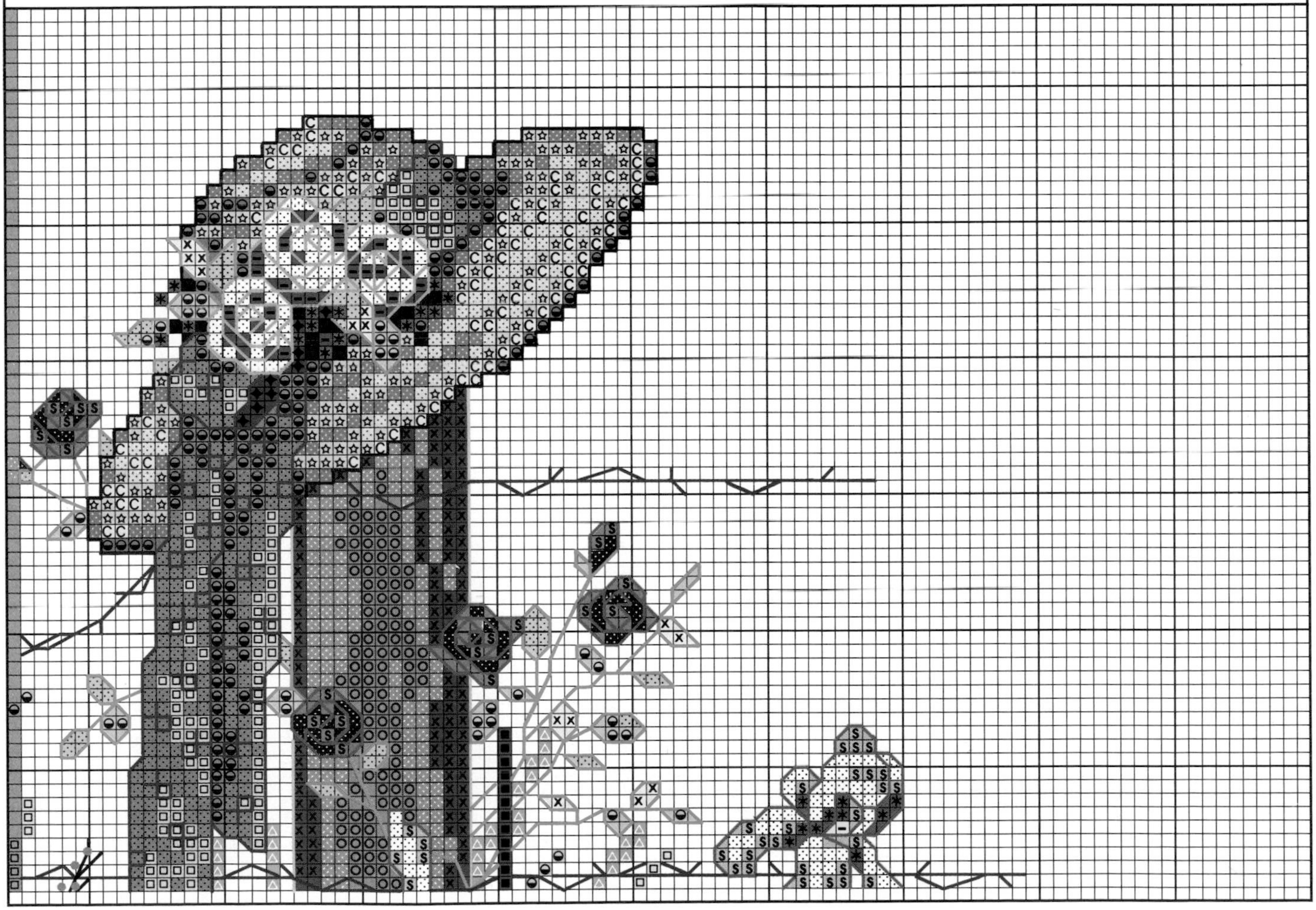

Continued on pages 18 and 19

For picnic basket, you will need a large basket, fabrics for lining and ruffle (see Steps 1 and 8 for amounts), fabric and $\frac{1}{8}$" dia. cord for cording (see Steps 1 and 3 for amounts), thread to match fabrics, polyester bonded batting, medium weight cardboard, wooden plaque (we used a 5" x 7" oval plaque), motifs cut from fabric (to decorate plaque), 2 coordinating colors of acrylic paint, matte Mod Podge® sealer, fine sandpaper, tack cloth, flat paintbrushes, hot glue gun, and glue sticks.

For an approx. 44" x 60" picnic cloth, you will need 1⅔ yds of 44"w fabric for picnic cloth, ½ yd of 44"w fabric for binding, and thread to match binding fabric.

For four 16" napkins, you will need four 17" squares of fabric and thread to match fabric.

PICNIC BASKET

1. To determine width of lining fabric, measure height of basket and add 4". To determine length of lining fabric, measure around basket at widest point and add 2". Cut a piece of lining fabric the determined measurements. Cut one 1"w bias strip of cording fabric (pieced as necessary) same length as lining fabric. Cut one 7"w strip of ruffle fabric (pieced as necessary) 2½ times the length of lining fabric.

2. For lining, press short edges of lining fabric ½" to wrong side.

3. For cording, press ends of bias strip ½" to wrong side. Cut a length of cord same length as bias strip. Lay cord along center on wrong side of strip. Matching long edges, fold strip over cord. Use a zipper foot and machine baste along length of strip close to cord. Whipstitch opening closed at each end.

4. Matching raw edges, baste cording along 1 long edge (top edge) on right side of lining.

5. For ruffle, match right sides and fold strip in half lengthwise. Use a ½" seam allowance and sew along each short edge. Cut corners diagonally; turn right side out. Matching raw edges, press ruffle flat. Baste ⅜" and ¼" from raw edge. Pull basting threads, drawing up gathers to fit top edge of lining.

6. Matching raw edges, baste ruffle along top edge on right side of lining. Using zipper foot and sewing as close as possible to cording, sew ruffle and cording to lining. Press seam allowance toward lining. Remove any visible basting threads.

7. (*Note:* Use hot glue for all gluing unless otherwise indicated.) With top edge of ruffle extending 1½" above top edge of basket, glue lining to inside of basket, overlapping short edges.

8. For padded bottom liner, place basket on cardboard and draw around bottom of basket. Cut out cardboard ¼" inside drawn line. Place cardboard in bottom of basket and trim to fit if necessary. Cut 1 piece of batting same size as cardboard. Cut 1 piece of lining fabric 1" larger on all sides than cardboard.

9. Center batting, then cardboard, on wrong side of fabric. Pulling fabric taut, glue edges of fabric to top (wrong side) of cardboard. Glue liner to inside bottom of basket, covering raw edge of lining.

10. (*Note:* Refer to photo for remaining steps.) For plaque, sand plaque and wipe lightly with tack cloth to remove dust. Use 1 color of paint to paint front of plaque; allow to dry. Use second color of paint to paint edge of plaque; allow to dry.

11. Arrange fabric motifs on plaque; use sealer to glue motifs in place. Allow to dry. Allowing to dry between coats, apply 2 coats of sealer to plaque.

12. Glue plaque to basket.

PICNIC CLOTH

1. Trim selvages from picnic cloth fabric.

2. For binding, cut one 1½"w bias strip of fabric 5⅞ yds long (pieced as necessary) from binding fabric. Press 1 end of strip ½" to wrong side. Matching wrong sides, press strip in half lengthwise; unfold. Press each long edge to center.

3. Beginning with unpressed end, match wrong side of center fold of binding to 1 raw edge of picnic cloth fabric (Fig. 1); pin binding to fabric, stopping at corner. Fold binding diagonally at corner and match center fold of binding to adjacent raw edge of fabric (Fig. 1).

Fig. 1

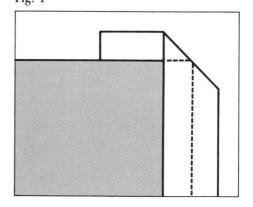

PICNIC SET (Continued)

4. Fold binding along center fold over raw edges of fabric, forming a mitered corner (Fig. 2); pin in place.

Fig. 2

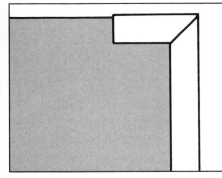

5. Repeating Steps 3 and 4, pin binding to all edges of fabric, overlapping ends. Stitching close to inner edge of binding, sew binding to fabric.

NAPKINS

1. For each napkin, press edges of each fabric square ¼" to wrong side; press ¼" to wrong side again.

2. To miter each corner, unfold corner and trim off a ⅜" triangle (Fig. 3a). Press trimmed corner ⅜" to wrong side (Fig. 3b).

Fig. 3a   Fig. 3b

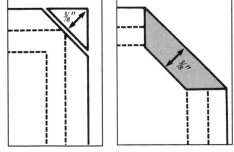

3. Refold edges of fabric. Stitch in place.

WILDFLOWER WEARABLES (Shown on page 11)

SHIRT

You will need a shirt (we used a ladies' white cotton shirt with hidden button placket), ribbons and laces, washable fabric glue or thread to match ribbons and laces, liquid fray preventative, small silk flowers, and safety pin.

1. Wash, dry, and press shirt, ribbons, and laces.

2. (*Note:* Refer to photo for Steps 2 and 3.) Arrange ribbons and laces on shirt, overlapping as desired and trimming to fit. Apply fray preventative to ribbon and lace ends; allow to dry. Glue or stitch ribbons and laces in place.

3. Tie desired ribbon into a bow around flowers; trim ends. Use safety pin on wrong side of shirt to pin flowers to shirt.

4. Remove flowers before laundering. If trims were glued in place, follow glue manufacturer's recommendations.

SHOES

You will need shoes (we used ladies' white canvas flats), wide and narrow satin ribbon, thread to match wide ribbon, 2 small sprays of silk flowers, masking tape, and washable fabric glue.

1. Measure width of shoe opening; add 4". Cut 2 lengths of wide ribbon the determined measurement. Measure around shoe opening; add 4". Cut 2 lengths of narrow ribbon the determined measurement.

2. (*Note:* Refer to photo and follow remaining steps for each shoe. Allow to dry after each glue step.) Press 1 end of 1 wide ribbon length ½" to wrong side. Arrange ribbon across toe of shoe with pressed edge even with 1 side of shoe opening; use tape across center of ribbon to hold ribbon in place. Wrap thread tightly around ribbon at remaining side of shoe opening; knot and trim thread ends. Trim ribbon end.

3. Beginning ¼" from 1 end of 1 narrow ribbon length, glue ribbon along pressed edge of wide ribbon. Fold short end of narrow ribbon to wrong side of wide ribbon; glue in place. Glue pressed edge of wide ribbon to shoe. Glue remainder of narrow ribbon around shoe opening, trimming ribbon even with knotted area of wide ribbon. Glue knotted area to shoe. Remove tape.

4. Tie 7" of narrow ribbon into a bow around 1 flower spray. Glue spray to shoe.

SUMMERY STRAW HAT
(Shown on page 10)

To decorate our wide-brimmed straw hat, we hot glued 1½"w purple plaid ribbon around the crown. We tied separate bows from 1"w white grosgrain ribbon and 1"w yellow satin ribbon. Separate double-loop bows were tied from 4"w white organdy ribbon, 1½"w purple plaid ribbon, and ⅝"w and ¼"w yellow satin ribbon. The bows were stacked together, largest to smallest, and a length of ⅝"w yellow satin ribbon was knotted around the bow centers. The bows were then hot glued to the back of the hat.

A sweet arrangement of silk flowers and greenery was hot glued around the right side of the hat. We began by grouping three white cabbage roses near the bow. Rosebuds and greenery were tucked in front of the roses along the crown of the hat. Old-fashioned velvet flowers and Johnny-jump-ups complete the arrangement, complementing the soft hues of the ribbons.

You will need a white V-neck jersey knit cardigan with button front and pockets, a white 13″ x 20″ oval Battenberg lace place mat, white lace trim same width as placket band of cardigan (see Step 2 for amount), embroidered handkerchiefs (we found ours at an antique shop), a purchased crocheted doily same width as cardigan pocket, 4 silk pansies, embroidery floss, three 20″ lengths of $\frac{1}{8}$″w satin ribbon for bows, ribbons and laces for trim on pockets, buttons (we used assorted sizes and colors of round and flower-shaped buttons), white thread, washable fabric glue (optional), tracing paper, lightweight fusible interfacing, paper-backed fusible web, liquid fray preventative, and 2 safety pins.

1. Wash, dry, and press cardigan, place mat, handkerchiefs, doily, lace, and ribbons. Remove buttons from cardigan.
2. For lace on neck and placket band, measure up 1 side of front opening, around neckline, and down remaining side of front opening; add 1″. Cut lace trim the determined measurement.
3. With $\frac{1}{2}$″ of lace extending beyond bottom edge of 1 side of front opening, pin lace along 1 side of front opening, neckline, and remaining side of front opening. Fold ends of lace to wrong side of cardigan; stitch or glue lace in place. Cut an opening in lace at each buttonhole. Apply fray preventative to all cut edges of lace. Allow to dry.
4. Sew desired buttons to cardigan to replace original buttons (we sewed small colored buttons on top of larger translucent buttons).

5. For lapels, press place mat in half diagonally (Fig. 1); cut place mat apart along pressed line. Turn 1 half of place mat over; use a pin to mark top side of each place mat half as right side.

Fig. 1

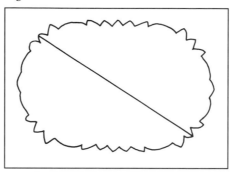

6. (*Note:* Refer to photo for Steps 6 - 15.) For right lapel, arrange 1 place mat half, marked side up, along cardigan neckline with raw edge extending at least 1$\frac{1}{2}$″ beyond neckline (Fig. 2); baste in place. If necessary, trim raw edge 1$\frac{1}{2}$″ from neckline. Press raw edge $\frac{1}{2}$″ to wrong side; press 1″ to inside of cardigan. Whipstitch pressed edge to inside of cardigan. Repeat for left lapel.

Fig. 2

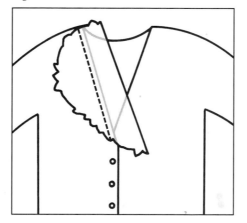

7. Stitching along inner edges of Battenberg lace, hand sew lapels to cardigan. If necessary, tack outer edges of Battenberg lace to cardigan to secure. Remove basting threads.
8. For heart appliqué pattern, trace heart pattern, page 23, onto tracing paper; cut out.
9. Follow manufacturers' instructions to fuse interfacing, then web, to wrong side of 1 handkerchief. For each appliqué, center pattern over desired motif on handkerchief; pin in place. Cut out heart. Place heart on cardigan; fuse in place. Use 1 strand of floss and whipstitch around edge of heart.
10. For doily pocket flap, cut doily in half; set aside 1 half for another use. Apply fray preventative to raw edge of remaining half; allow to dry. Press raw edge (top) $\frac{1}{2}$″ to wrong side; press $\frac{1}{2}$″ to wrong side again. Insert pressed edge of doily into 1 pocket; whipstitch pressed edge to inside of pocket.
11. For handkerchief pocket flap, cut 1 corner from handkerchief with raw edge (top) 2″ longer than width of pocket. Matching raw edges, press top corners of handkerchief corner 1″ to wrong side. Press raw edge $\frac{1}{2}$″ to wrong side; press $\frac{1}{2}$″ to wrong side again. Insert pressed edge of handkerchief corner into remaining pocket; whipstitch pressed edge to inside of pocket.
12. For lace flower on handkerchief pocket flap, cut a 10″ length of desired lace (we used 1$\frac{1}{2}$″w lace). Overlap ends of lace $\frac{1}{2}$″ and sew together. Baste $\frac{1}{8}$″ from long straight edge of lace. Pull basting thread, gathering lace tightly; knot thread and trim ends.

BATTENBERG LACE CARDIGAN (Continued)

For bow, thread a needle with 1 length of ⅛"w ribbon. Take needle down through center of lace circle from front to back, leaving 10" of ribbon at front; bring needle back up ⅛" away. Thread a button onto ribbon ends. Tie ribbon ends into a bow. Tack flower to pocket flap.

13. For bow on doily pocket flap, tie remaining ⅛"w ribbon lengths together into a bow. Tack bow to doily pocket flap.

14. For each pansy pin, remove petals from 2 flower centers. Layer petals together. Sewing petals together, sew a button to center of petals. Use a safety pin on wrong side of cardigan to pin pansy to cardigan.

15. Arrange additional buttons, lace, and ribbons on cardigan as desired; apply fray preventative to all raw edges. Stitch or glue in place.

16. To launder, remove pansy pins and hand wash; hang to dry.

WILDFLOWER BASKET
(Shown on page 11)

A 14" dia. moss-covered basket holds a sunny arrangement of our favorite wildflowers. We filled the basket to within 1" of the rim with floral foam and secured the foam with glue. A layer of sheet moss covering the foam was secured with florist's greening pins, although glue can be used.

We arranged a variety of silk wildflowers in the basket, using taller stems in the back and shorter stems toward the front. Some of the larger wildflowers include black-eyed Susans, coreopsis, bells of Ireland, and pink mini roses. The front of the basket is filled with African violets, and a small robin's nest with eggs inside is tucked among the flowers.

Silk field buttons, prickly lettuce, and tiny white, yellow, and purple field flowers add color, while preserved tree fern and dried mini oak are used to fill in among the flowers. An artificial monarch butterfly lights among the flowers, providing a lively touch.

PRESSED FLOWER PICTURE
(Shown on page 14)

You will need fresh flowers and leaves (blossoms should be no more than ¼" thick; we used pansies, herb leaves, and wildflowers), a flower press (or a thick catalog, heavy books, and facial tissue), watercolor paper, tweezers, craft glue, matte clear acrylic spray, frame, and wired ribbon.

1. (*Note:* Use a flower press to press flowers, or follow Steps 1 - 4.) Open catalog at center and cover 1 page with tissue.
2. (*Note:* Avoid using flowers that are damp, wilted, or have broken parts.) Trim flower stems very close to blossoms. Without allowing flowers or leaves to touch, place flowers and leaves flat on tissue; cover with a second layer of tissue.
3. Close catalog and place in a dry, well-ventilated area. Weight with books. Leave catalog weighted for 10 to 14 days, allowing flowers to dry.
4. Open catalog and carefully remove top layer of tissue.
5. For flower arrangement, cut watercolor paper to fit in frame. Referring to photo, use tweezers to arrange pressed flowers on watercolor paper; use small dots of glue to secure. Allow to dry.
6. Lightly spray flowers with acrylic spray. Allow to dry.
7. Insert arrangement into frame.
8. Tie ribbon into a bow; trim ends. Arrange bow and streamers on frame; glue to secure. Allow to dry.

FLOWER GARDEN AFGHAN (Shown on page 13)

FINISHED SIZE: approx. 45" x 70"

SUPPLIES

Worsted Weight Yarn, approx.:
MC (Ecru) – 21 ounces (600 grams, 1325 yards)
Color A (Yellow) – 3 ounces (90 grams, 190 yards)
Color B (Lt green *and/or* dk green) – 8 ounces (230 grams, 505 yards) *total*
Color C (Pink) – 2½ ounces (70 grams, 160 yards)
CC (Scraps) – 14 ounces (400 grams, 880 yards) *total*
Note: Each motif requires approx. 5 yards of CC for Rnd 2 and 7 yards of CC for Rnd 3.
Crochet hook, size F (4.00 mm) *or* size needed for gauge
Yarn needle

ABBREVIATIONS

Beg	Beginning
CC	Contrasting Color
ch	chain
dc	double crochet(s)
MC	Main Color
Rnd(s)	Round(s)
sc	single crochet(s)
sp(s)	space(s)
st	stitches
YO	yarn over

★ – work instructions following ★ as many *more* times as indicated in addition to the first time.
( ) – work enclosed instructions *as many* times as specified by the number immediately following *or* work all enclosed instructions in the stitch or space indicated *or* contains explanatory remarks.

GAUGE: Rnds 1 and 2 = 3" (DO NOT HESITATE TO CHANGE HOOK SIZE TO OBTAIN CORRECT GAUGE.)

STITCHES

Beginning Cluster: Working all in the same sp (YO, insert hook in sp and draw up loop, YO, draw through 2 loops on hook) twice, YO, draw through all 3 loops on hook.

Cluster: Working all in the same sp (YO, insert hook in sp and draw up loop, YO, draw through 2 loops on hook) 3 times, YO, draw through all 4 loops on hook.

Reverse Single Crochet: Working from *left* to *right*, ch 1, ★ insert hook in st to right of hook (Fig. 1a), YO and draw through, under and to left of loop on hook (Fig. 1b) (2 loops on hook), YO and draw through both loops on hook (Fig. 1c); repeat from ★ around.

Fig. 1a

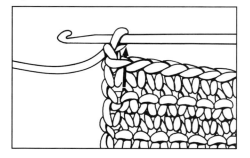

Fig. 1b

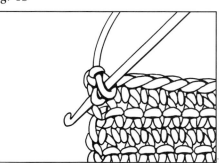

Fig. 1c

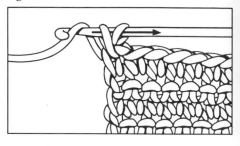

MOTIF (Make 67)

With Color A ch 6, join with slip st to form a ring.

Rnd 1: Ch 3, work Beg Cluster in ring, ch 3, ★ work Cluster in ring, ch 3; repeat from ★ 4 times more; join with slip st to top of Beg Cluster, finish off: 6 Clusters.

Rnd 2: Join CC with slip st in first ch-3 sp, ch 3, work (Beg Cluster, ch 3, Cluster) in same ch-3 sp, ch 3, ★ work (Cluster, ch 3, Cluster) in next ch-3 sp, ch 3; repeat from ★ around; join with slip st to top of Beg Cluster, finish off: 12 Clusters.

Rnd 3: Join CC with slip st in last ch-3 sp made, ch 3, work Beg Cluster in same ch-3 sp, ch 3, work (Cluster, ch 3, Cluster) in next ch-3 sp, ch 3, ★ work Cluster in next ch-3 sp, ch 3, work (Cluster, ch 3, Cluster) in next ch-3 sp, ch 3; repeat from ★ around; join with slip st to top of Beg Cluster, finish off: 18 Clusters.

Rnd 4: Join Color B with slip st in last ch-3 sp made, ch 3 *(counts as first dc, now and throughout)*, dc in same ch-3 sp, 2 dc in next ch-3 sp, (2 dc, ch 2, 2 dc) in next ch-3 sp, ★ 2 dc in each of next 2 ch-3 sps, (2 dc, ch 2, 2 dc) in next ch-3 sp; repeat from ★ around; join with slip st to first dc, finish off: 48 dc.

FLOWER GARDEN AFGHAN
(Continued)

Rnd 5: Join MC with slip st in first ch-2 sp, ch 3, 2 dc in same ch-2 sp, dc in next 8 dc, ★ 3 dc in next ch-2 sp, dc in next 8 dc; repeat from ★ around; join with slip st to first dc: 66 dc.

Rnd 6: Ch 3, 4 dc in next dc, ★ dc in next 10 dc, 4 dc in next dc; repeat from ★ around to last 9 dc, dc in last 9 dc; join with slip st to first dc, finish off: 84 dc.

JOINING
Refer to Diagram for placement of motifs. With right sides together, sew motifs together through back loops only.

EDGING
With right side facing, join Color C with slip st in any st. Work Reverse Sc in each st and 2 Reverse Sc in each corner around; join with slip st to first st, finish off. Weave in all yarn ends.

DIAGRAM

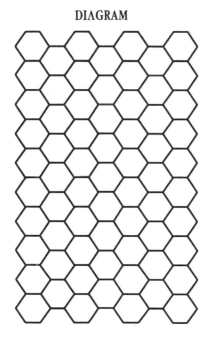

MARBLEIZED STATIONERY (Shown on page 14)

You will need 1 gallon liquid starch, one 12" x 18" disposable aluminum foil roasting pan, acrylic paints (we used pink, purple, yellow, and green), paper towels, waxed paper, craft glue, buttons, and ribbons.

For note cards and envelopes, you will also need plain white paper, purchased note cards and envelopes, and paper-backed fusible web.

For stationery folder, you will also need an 11" x 17" piece of light-colored watercolor paper, coordinating thread, and two 10" lengths of $\frac{1}{16}$"w satin ribbon.

NOTE CARDS AND ENVELOPES
1. (*Note:* For marbleized paper, follow Steps 1 - 6.) Pour starch into pan to a depth of 1".
2. To apply paint to starch surface, hold bottle of paint near surface and gently squeeze out a small dot of paint (paint will float and begin to spread). Repeat to apply several dots of each color of paint. Remove dots that do not spread with a fingertip or the corner of a paper towel.
3. To form marble design, use a fork or the wooden end of a paintbrush to move paint around on surface of starch, forming desired patterns.
4. Gently place a piece of plain white paper on starch surface (paper will float); immediately pick up paper by 2 corners and lay paper, painted side up, on a layer of paper towels. Using dry paper towels, blot excess starch and paint from paper. Lay paper on waxed paper; allow to dry.
5. After marbleizing each sheet of paper, remove any excess paint from starch in pan by placing a layer of paper towels on starch surface. Lift towels from starch and discard.
6. Use a warm dry iron to press marbleized paper.
7. Following manufacturer's instructions, fuse web to unpainted side of paper.
8. (*Note:* Refer to photo for remaining steps.) For each note card, cut a piece of marbleized paper $\frac{1}{4}$" smaller on all sides than front of note card. Fuse paper to note card. Tie 2 ribbon lengths together into a bow. Arrange bow and buttons on note card; glue in place.
9. For each envelope, cut a piece of marbleized paper same size as opened envelope. Place paper in envelope, trimming side edges to fit if necessary. Trim paper to expose gummed edge of envelope. Fuse paper inside envelope.

STATIONERY FOLDER
1. Using watercolor paper, follow Steps 1 - 6 of Note Cards and Envelopes instructions to make one $8\frac{1}{2}$" x $16\frac{1}{2}$" piece of marbleized paper.
2. For pocket, fold 1 short edge of paper 5" to wrong side. For top edge, fold remaining short edge $\frac{3}{4}$" to wrong side.
3. Using a medium width zigzag stitch with a medium stitch length, sew $\frac{1}{4}$" from edges of paper, stitching through both layers where necessary.
4. For flap, fold top edge of paper $3\frac{1}{4}$" to wrong side.
5. For ribbon closure, thread a large needle with 1 length of $\frac{1}{16}$"w ribbon; knot 1 end. Coming up through flap from back to front, thread ribbon through center of flap $\frac{1}{4}$" from edge. Repeat to thread remaining ribbon length through center of pocket $1\frac{1}{2}$" from top edge of pocket. Tie ribbons into a bow.
6. Referring to photo, arrange ribbon(s) and buttons on flap; glue in place.

Chart, page 34

Thoughts of Spring

We can almost hear the hum of the sewing machine
and the whir of its treadle when we enter the world reflected
in Paula's Thoughts of Spring. As our imaginations transport us
back in time, we can share the tingle of excitement that the young
needlewoman must have felt in anticipation of wearing her
beautiful new spring dresses. Her pleasure in her handiwork is
evident in the attention she has given to every detail —
ruffles of lace on the bodice of one, a ribbon sash for the fitted
waistline of another. The nostalgic projects in this collection
are meant to bring us a special sense of closeness to our sister
from the past. Featuring old-fashioned sewing notions or
echoing lovely images of yesteryear, these accents and
accessories link us to a gentle time that's delightful to recall.

In years gone by, young girls often practiced their dressmaking skills by sewing for their dolls. This little doll, clad in our old-time dress, can be arranged with a collection of vintage sewing accoutrements to adorn a quiet corner in your sewing room. Tied with a satin ribbon, the pretty pincushion would have been right at home in Grandmother's sewing basket.

Pincushion, page 41
Doll Dress, page 42

*B*its and pieces of the past — snippets of lace and ribbon, antique buttons, and other articles — make lovely trims for sewing accessories. The needlework carrier helps organize patterns and supplies, and the chatelaine keeps needles and scissors close at hand.

Needlework Carrier, page 44
Needleworker's Chatelaine, page 41

A Seamstress' Wreath, page 43

$\mathcal{S}$weet old-fashioned roses lend an air of romance to our everyday lives. A grapevine wreath adorned with these lovely blossoms and vintage sewing notions frames a collection of antique dress patterns, providing a precious link to seamstresses of the past. An ordinary wooden box becomes a beautiful keepsake chest when embellished with sculpted clay trim and a padded lid of rose-print fabric.

Keepsake Box, page 39

You can create a captivating vignette right out of one of Paula's paintings by embellishing miniature wooden furniture and other collectibles. Here, a tiny armoire and ladderback chair take on turn-of-the-century charm.

Sewing Room Vignette, page 38

*A*dorned with feminine trimmings, a drawer from an antique sewing machine cabinet provides a nostalgic setting for an assortment of sewing memorabilia. What appears to be a pair of elegantly bound books is really a pretty box to hold sewing supplies, keepsakes, or jewelry.

Book Box, page 40
Grandma's Sewing Drawer, page 45

THOUGHTS OF SPRING (Shown on page 26)

X	DMC	¼X	B'ST	COLOR	X	DMC	¼X	B'ST	COLOR	X	DMC	¼X	½X	B'ST	COLOR
	blanc			white		502	¼X	★	blue green	★	782	¼X		°	dk gold
○	ecru			ecru	−	503	¼X		lt blue green	C	783	¼X			gold
◆	310	¼X	*	black	+	504			vy lt blue green	V	801	¼X			brown
✳	316			lt rose	△	543			vy lt beige brown		814			†	vy dk red
✕	347	¼X	*	lt red	□	642	¼X	‡	lt brown grey	■	815	¼X			dk red
▲	420	¼X		vy dk yellow	✳	644	¼X		vy lt brown grey	C	822				lt beige
	433	¼X	†	lt brown	◆	645			dk grey		840	¼X		+	dk beige brown
S	434	¼X		vy dk tan		646	¼X		grey		841	¼X	△		beige brown
✕	435	¼X		dk tan	−	676			lt yellow	S	842	¼X	⊖		lt beige brown
	436	¼X		tan	□	677			vy lt yellow		844	¼X			vy dk grey
+	437	¼X		lt tan		680	¼X		dk yellow		869			§	dk khaki
■	451	¼X	+	dk grey violet	△	704	¼X	§	yellow green		898			°	dk brown
	452		+	grey violet	☆	729			yellow	+	927		★		grey blue
☆	453			lt grey violet	V	738	¼X	*	vy lt tan		930				dk blue
	498	¼X		red		760	¼X		salmon	◆	931	¼X			blue
	500		★	vy dk blue green	S	761	¼X		lt salmon	S	932	¼X	✳	§	lt blue
○	501		★	dk blue green	⊖	762			vy lt grey	◆	987	¼X		†	dk green

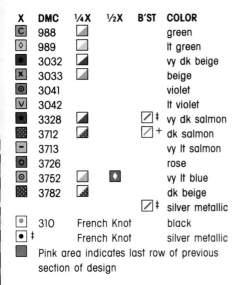

X	DMC	¼X	½X	B'ST	COLOR
C	988	◪			green
◊	989	◪			lt green
★	3032	◪			vy dk beige
✕	3033	◪			beige
◉	3041				violet
V	3042				lt violet
▲	3328	◪		☑ ‡	vy dk salmon
⊡	3712	◪		☑ +	dk salmon
−	3713				vy lt salmon
○	3726				rose
◉	3752	◪	◈		vy lt blue
▨	3782	◪			dk beige
				☑ ‡	silver metallic
⊡	310	French Knot			black
⬤ ‡		French Knot			silver metallic
▨	Pink area indicates last row of previous section of design				

Note: Mirror reflection and wallpaper stitched with **1** strand of floss.

* Black for hanger, hanging rod, sewing machine, and base. Use 2 strands of black for "SINGER". Lt red for dress. Vy lt tan for all other.

† Lt brown for dress form and armoire. Dk green for white dress and hat on floor. Vy dk red for all other.

+ Dk grey violet for hat and sampler. Grey violet for dresses. Dk salmon for quilt. Dk beige brown for all other.

★ Vy dk blue green for chair. Dk blue green for roses in window. Blue green for all other.

‡ Lt brown grey for curtains, quilt, hatbox, and sampler in mirror. Vy dk salmon for roses. Kreinik Balger® Cord #001C silver for all other.

§ Yellow green for sewing machine detail. Dk khaki for hats and basket. Lt blue for quilt.

° Dk gold for brooches on dresses and lettering on sewing machine. Dk brown for all other.

THOUGHTS OF SPRING (180w x 148h)			
14 count	12⅞"	x	10⅝"
16 count	11¼"	x	9¼"
18 count	10"	x	8¼"
22 count	8¼"	x	6¾"

Thoughts of Spring (180w x 148h) was stitched over 2 fabric threads on a 22" x 20" piece of Cream Belfast Linen (32 ct). Two strands of floss were used for Cross Stitch and 1 for Backstitch unless otherwise noted. The design was custom framed.

Continued on pages 36 and 37

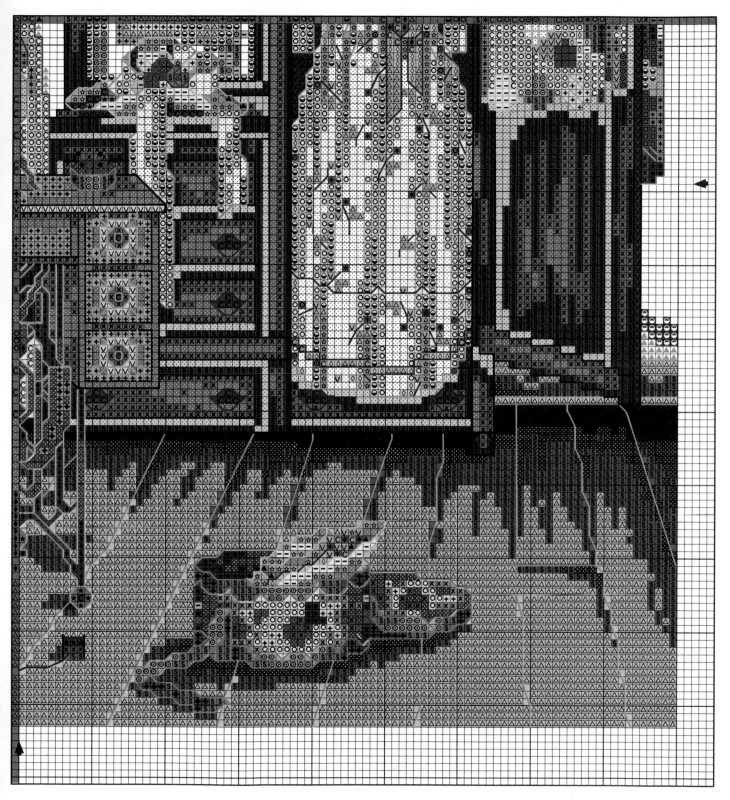

37

SEWING ROOM VIGNETTE (Shown on page 32)

For armoire, you will need one 8"w x 12"h x 3½"d unfinished wooden armoire and floral rub-on transfers (available at craft stores), lt brown acrylic paint, wooden peg for door hanger, shank buttons to replace original drawer pulls (optional), hot glue gun, and glue sticks.

For chair, you will need one 7½"h unfinished wooden chair (available at craft stores), green acrylic paint, fabric for chair pad, 1"w pregathered lace trim, 16" of ⅜"w ribbon, and thread to match fabric.

For armoire and chair, you will also need fine sandpaper, tack cloth, foam brushes, brown waterbase stain, a soft cloth, and matte clear acrylic spray.

For accessories, you will need small boxes with lids (we used 3" dia. round, 2" x 3" oval, and 3"w hexagonal boxes), fabrics and trims to cover boxes, lid from a 2" dia. box for embroidery hoop, a small piece of embroidered fabric (we found ours at an antique shop), tagboard (manila folder), Design Master® glossy wood tone spray (available at craft stores), threaded needle to place in hoop, miniature scissors, small basket, fabrics and lightweight cardboard for fabric bolts, 4" dia. straw hat, flowers to decorate hat, 3" high teddy bear, ribbons to decorate hat and bear, craft glue, fabric marking pencil, and additional small or miniature items (we used doilies, ribbons, artificial flowers, carded buttons, thread spools, basket, teapot, and books).

ARMOIRE
1. If desired, remove original pulls from drawer(s). Glue peg inside 1 door for hanger.

2. Sand armoire and wipe lightly with tack cloth to remove dust.

3. Paint armoire lt brown; allow to dry.

4. Referring to photo and following manufacturer's instructions, apply rub-on transfers to armoire. Spray armoire lightly with acrylic spray; allow to dry.

5. Working on 1 section at a time, use a damp foam brush to apply stain to armoire; use soft cloth to wipe away excess. Allow to dry.

6. Allowing to dry between coats, apply 2 coats of acrylic spray to armoire.

7. If original pulls were removed, glue buttons to drawer(s) for pulls.

CHAIR
1. Using green paint, follow Steps 2, 3, 5, and 6 of Armoire instructions to paint and antique chair.

2. For chair pad, measure length and width of seat. Cut 2 pieces of fabric the determined measurements. Measure around edge of seat; add ½". Cut lace the determined measurement.

3. With right sides facing, match straight edge of lace to raw edge of 1 fabric piece; baste in place.

4. Matching right sides and raw edges and leaving an opening for turning, use a ¼" seam allowance to sew fabric pieces together. Cut corners diagonally, turn right side out, and press. Sew final closure by hand.

5. Cut ribbon in half. Tack center of 1 ribbon length to each back corner of chair pad. Tie chair pad to chair.

ACCESSORIES
1. (*Note:* Allow to dry after each glue step. Follow Steps 1 - 5 to cover each box.) To cover sides of box, measure around box and add ½"; measure height of box and add ¼". Cut a fabric strip the determined measurements.

2. With 1 long edge of fabric strip even with top edge of box, glue strip around box, overlapping ends.

3. At ¼" intervals, clip fabric extending beyond bottom of box to within 1/16" of box edge. Glue clipped edges of fabric to bottom of box.

4. To cover lid, use fabric marking pencil to draw around lid on wrong side of fabric. Cut out fabric ¼" outside pencil line. At ¼" intervals, clip edges of fabric to within 1/16" of pencil line.

5. Center lid on wrong side of fabric. Alternating sides and pulling fabric taut, glue clipped edges of fabric to side of lid. Glue desired trims around side of lid. If desired, glue a doily to top of lid.

6. For embroidery hoop in basket, cut a 5" dia. circle from embroidered fabric. Insert threaded needle near center of circle. Center circle on top of 2" dia. lid; glue in place. Smooth fabric over side of lid and glue in place. Cut a ⅜" x 6½" strip of tagboard. Spray strip with wood tone spray; allow to dry. Glue strip around side of lid. Glue scissors to fabric. Place hoop in basket.

7. For each bolt of fabric, cut a 1½" x 3¾" piece from cardboard. Cut a 6¾" x 9" strip of fabric. Press long edges of fabric strip 1½" to wrong side. Glue 1 end of pressed fabric strip along 1 long edge of cardboard piece. Wrap fabric around cardboard. Glue remaining end of strip in place.

8. For hat, tie a length of ribbon into a bow around crown of hat. Glue flowers to hat over bow.

9. For bear, tie a length of ribbon into a bow around bear's neck.

10. Arrange covered boxes, needlework basket, fabric bolts, hat, bear, and other items in and around armoire and chair.

KEEPSAKE BOX   (Shown on page 31)

You will need a wooden box with flat area large enough to accommodate 18″ x 6½″ design, natural Maché Clay no-bake sculpting compound, Folk Art® Wicker White and Barn Wood acrylic paint and Apple Butter Brown Antiquing, Delta Home Decor Cactus Green Pickling Gel, fabric and purchased ⅜″ dia. cording for padded lid (see Steps 12 and 14 for amounts), medium weight cardboard, high-loft polyester bonded batting, dull knife, small paintbrush, waxed paper, foam brushes, fine sandpaper, matte clear acrylic spray, soft cloths, tracing paper, rolling pin, utility scissors, hot glue gun, glue sticks, ballpoint pen, and tack cloth.

1. Trace patterns onto tracing paper; cut out.
2. Working on waxed paper, use rolling pin to roll out clay to ¼″ thickness.
3. Place patterns on clay and use pen to draw around patterns for indicated numbers of pieces. Use scissors to cut out pieces. Place pieces on waxed paper and smooth cut edges.
4. (*Note:* Refer to photo for remaining steps.) For details on each clay piece, place pattern on piece and use pen to draw over lines and dots, lightly pressing details into piece. Remove pattern. Use knife and wooden end of small paintbrush to press lines and dots into piece.
5. For basket handle, roll out two 9″ long, ⅛″ dia. lengths of clay. Twist lengths together. Bend twisted lengths into handle shape; press ends onto top corners of basket.
6. Allow clay pieces to dry overnight on waxed paper.
7. Sand box and wipe lightly with tack cloth to remove dust. Glue clay pieces to front of box.
8. Mix 1 part Wicker White and 1 part Barn Wood paint. Allowing to dry between coats, apply 2 coats of paint mixture to box, including clay pieces. If necessary, sand wood between coats, being careful not to sand clay pieces.
9. Allowing to dry between coats, apply 2 coats of acrylic spray to box.
10. Follow manufacturer's instructions to apply pickling gel to box.
11. Working on 1 section at a time, use a damp foam brush to apply antiquing to box; use a soft cloth to wipe away excess. Allow to dry.
12. For padded lid, cut a piece of cardboard slightly smaller than lid, rounding off corners. Cut 2 pieces of batting same size as cardboard. Cut 1 piece of fabric 2″ larger on all sides than cardboard.
13. Center both layers of batting, then cardboard, on wrong side of fabric. Alternating sides and pulling fabric taut, glue edges of fabric to back of cardboard.
14. Measure around edge of padded shape; add 1″. Cut a length of cording the determined measurement. Glue seam allowance of cording along edge on wrong side of padded shape, trimming cording to fit exactly.
15. Glue padded shape to lid.

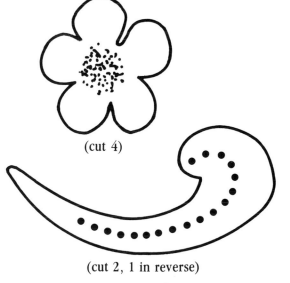

(cut 1)

(cut 1)

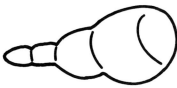

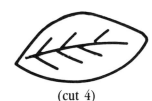

(cut 4)

(cut 2, 1 in reverse)

(cut 2, 1 in reverse)

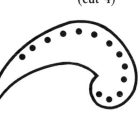

(cut 2, 1 in reverse)

(cut 4)

(cut 2, 1 in reverse)

BOOK BOX (Shown on page 33)

You will need an 8⅜"w x 2½"h x 5⅜"d cardboard school box, metallic gold spray paint, two 8½" x 10½" fabric pieces to cover box, 2 yds of ⅛" dia. satin rattail cord to coordinate with fabric, ⅛" thick foam board or cardboard, heavy paper, cream-colored paper, metallic gold pen with fine point, items to decorate book spines (we used 1⅜"w tapestry ribbon, colored paper, and ⅜"w gold trim), craft knife, spray adhesive, and craft glue.

1. Spray paint inside and outside of box; allow to dry.
2. (*Note:* Refer to photo for remaining steps. Use craft glue unless otherwise indicated. Allow to dry after each glue step.) To form "spines" of books, cut a 4" x 8½" strip from heavy paper. Fold paper in half lengthwise. Referring to Fig. 1, glue fold of paper to center back of box.

Fig. 1

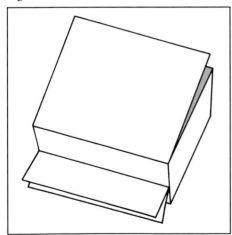

3. Referring to Fig. 2, bend each long edge of paper toward box. With lid of box closed and each long edge of paper overlapping edge of box ¼", glue long edges of paper to box.

Fig. 2

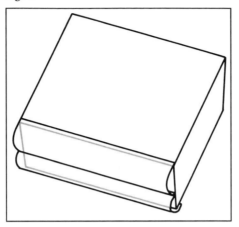

4. Use craft knife to cut two 5½" x 8½" pieces from foam board.
5. For each book "cover," place 1 fabric piece right side down on a protected flat surface; apply spray adhesive to wrong side. Referring to Fig. 3, place 1 foam board piece on fabric with 1 long edge (front edge) of board 1" from 1 long edge (front edge) of fabric. Fold 2 closest corners of fabric diagonally over board (Fig. 3). Fold front edge, then side edges, over board, pressing fabric together where it extends past board. Leave remaining long edge (back edge) of fabric free.

Fig. 3

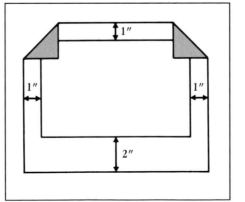

6. With back edge of fabric extending toward spines, center 1 cover right side up on top of box with back edge of foam board even with back edge of box; glue in place. Smooth extending fabric over top book spine and glue in place, trimming fabric to fit if necessary. Repeat to glue remaining cover to bottom of box and remaining book spine.
7. For book "pages," cut one 2½" x 8⅜" piece and two 2½" x 6" pieces of cream-colored paper. Use a ruler and gold pen to draw lines lengthwise on paper pieces to resemble gilded pages of a book.
8. Trimming paper to fit, use spray adhesive to secure 2½" x 8⅜" lined paper piece to front of box.
9. For each side of box, place one 2½" x 6" lined paper piece on side of box with 1 short edge even with front of box; trim remaining short edge to fit into arches of book spines. Use spray adhesive to secure paper to side of box.
10. For book spine decorations, glue ribbon, paper, and trim to box. If desired, use gold pen to draw designs on spine.
11. Glue 2 lengths of cord between book spines. Glue 2 lengths of cord along tops of spines, down center of pages, and along bottoms of spines.

PINCUSHION

(Shown on page 28)

You will need one 4″ dia. x 1¾″h Shaker box (without lid), one 4″ dia. plastic foam ball, one 10½″ square of velvet fabric, one 11½″ square each of floral fabric and lining fabric, regular sewing thread and heavy thread (buttonhole twist) to match fabric, 30″ of ½″w satin ribbon, polyester fiberfill, paring knife, craft glue, compass, and tracing paper.

1. For patterns, use compass to draw one 9½″ dia. circle and one 10½″ dia. circle on tracing paper; cut out.
2. Use patterns and cut one 9½″ dia. circle from velvet and one 10½″ dia. circle each from floral and lining fabrics.
3. Use knife to cut 1″ from foam ball, forming a flat surface (bottom). Center and glue velvet circle over rounded part (top) of ball, smoothing wrinkles as necessary. Secure with pins until dry.
4. Glue foam ball into Shaker box.
5. Matching right sides and raw edges and leaving an opening for turning, use a ¼″ seam allowance to sew remaining fabric circles together. Clip seam allowance, turn right side out, and press. Sew final closure by hand.
6. Using heavy thread, baste ⅝″ from edge of fabric circle. Center box on lining. Place a 1″ dia. roll of fiberfill on lining around box. Pull basting thread, gathering circle around fiberfill and box; knot thread and trim ends. Glue lining to rim of box along basting line.
7. Tie a knot at center of ribbon. Tie a knot 3″ from each side of center knot. Tie ribbon into a bow around pincushion, covering basting thread. Use dots of glue behind knots and bow to secure.

NEEDLEWORKER'S CHATELAINE

(Shown on page 29)

You will need 1 approx. 13½″ x 19″ reversible quilted fabric place mat with binding, floral motifs cut from fabric, one 4″ x 8″ piece of floral fabric for needle case lining, one 2″ x 2½″ piece of felt to coordinate with lining fabric, assorted buttons, thread to match place mat, 32″ each of 1″w grosgrain ribbon and 1″w tapestry ribbon, purchased 3½″ dia. doily, 8″ of 2″w flat lace, 5″ of 1¼″w flat lace, 30″ of ⅜″w satin ribbon, seam ripper, tracing paper, and fabric glue.

1. Use seam ripper to remove binding from place mat. Set binding aside.
2. (*Note:* Follow Steps 2 - 9 for scissors carrier.) For back pattern, trace pink outline of pattern onto tracing paper. For pocket pattern, trace grey area of pattern onto tracing paper. Cut out patterns.
3. Use patterns and cut 1 back and 1 pocket from place mat.
4. Stitch along flap fold line of back where indicated by dotted line on pattern.
5. To bind top of pocket, cut a 3¼″ length from place mat binding. Insert short straight edge (top) of pocket piece between folded edges of binding; stitch binding to pocket along previous stitching line.
6. Matching bottom and side edges, baste back and pocket pieces together.
7. To bind edges of carrier, cut a 17″ length from place mat binding. Open 1 end of binding and press ½″ to wrong side; refold binding. Beginning with unpressed end of binding, insert edges of carrier between long folded edges of binding. Stitch binding to carrier along previous stitching line.

8. (*Note:* Refer to photo for remaining steps. Allow to dry after each glue step.) For ties, cut two 6″ lengths of ⅜″w ribbon. Press 1 end of each length ½″ to 1 side. With carrier open, whipstitch pressed end of 1 tie to center top edge of flap on inside of carrier. With carrier closed, whipstitch pressed end of remaining tie to pocket opposite tie on flap.
9. Glue doily and buttons to carrier.
10. (*Note:* Follow Steps 10 - 15 for needle case.) Cut a 4″ x 8″ piece from place mat. Glue 2″w lace lengthwise along center on 1 side (right side) of place mat piece. Place place mat piece and lining fabric piece wrong sides together; baste close to edges.
11. For center fold line, match short edges and press needle case in half; unfold. Stitch along pressed line.
12. Glue 1¼″w lace diagonally across top left corner of lining; trim lace even with edge of case. For needle holder, center felt piece on right half of lining; glue top ½″ of felt piece in place.
13. Cut a 25″ length from binding and repeat Step 7 to bind edges of needle case, mitering binding at corners.
14. For ties, cut an 18″ length of ⅜″w ribbon. Center ribbon lengthwise over lace on outside of needle case; glue in place.
15. Glue floral motifs and buttons to inside and outside of needle case.
16. For chatelaine, glue 1″w ribbon lengths wrong sides together. Press ends ½″ to 1 side (right side). With right side of ribbon facing back of scissors carrier, securely sew 1″ at 1 end of ribbon to carrier. Repeat to attach remaining end of ribbon to back of needle case.

DOLL DRESS (Shown on page 28)

For dress to fit a 14" tall doll, you will need ½ yd of 44"w fabric for dress; a 10" square of fabric for yoke; ⅓ yd of ⅛"w and 2" of ⅜"w satin ribbon, ½ yd of ⅜"w lace trim, and 7" of 1"w flat lace (for yoke trim, cuff trim, and collar); ⅔ yd of ⅜"w satin ribbon for sash; thread to match dress fabric; one ½"w cameo shank button with shank removed; small artificial flowers; snaps; paper-backed fusible web; tracing paper; and fabric glue.

1. For bodice patterns, trace pink outlines of patterns, page 43, onto tracing paper. For yoke patterns, trace blue areas of patterns, page 43, onto tracing paper. Cut out patterns. For sleeve pattern, page 43, follow Tracing Patterns, page 124.

2. Following manufacturer's instructions, fuse web to wrong side of yoke fabric.

3. Using patterns, cut 1 yoke front and 2 yoke backs (1 in reverse) from yoke fabric. Cut 1 bodice front, 2 bodice backs (1 in reverse), and 2 sleeves from dress fabric.

4. Fuse yoke pieces to bodice pieces where indicated by blue areas on patterns.

5. For trims on yoke front, cut one 2" length of 1"w lace and two 2" lengths of ⅛"w ribbon.

6. (*Note:* Refer to photo for remaining steps. Allow to dry after each glue step.) Glue 1"w lace to center of yoke front. Glue 2" length of ⅜"w ribbon to center of lace. Glue ⅛"w ribbon lengths ⅛" from each side of lace. Trim ribbons and lace even with top edge of yoke.

7. Press straight edge (bottom) of each sleeve ¼" to wrong side; glue in place.

8. For trim on each sleeve, cut one 3" length each of ⅜"w lace and ⅛"w ribbon. Glue right side of lace to wrong side of sleeve with edge of lace extending ¼" beyond bottom of sleeve. Matching 1 long edge of ribbon to bottom of sleeve, glue ribbon to right side of sleeve.

9. (*Note:* Use a ¼" seam allowance for Steps 9 - 22 unless otherwise indicated.) For bodice, match right sides and raw edges and sew bodice backs to bodice front at shoulders. Press seams open.

10. To gather top edge of each sleeve, baste ¼" and ⅛" from edge between ★'s shown on pattern. Pull basting threads, gathering edge of sleeve to fit armhole edge of bodice.

11. Matching right sides and raw edges, sew 1 sleeve to each armhole edge of bodice (Fig. 1).

Fig. 1

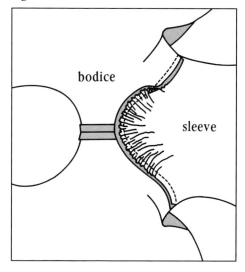

bodice

sleeve

12. Matching right sides and raw edges, sew side and sleeve seams. Turn right side out and press.

13. For yoke ruffle, cut a 1¼" x 30" strip from dress fabric. Use a narrow width zigzag stitch with a short stitch length to stitch ⅛" from 1 long edge of strip. Trim seam allowance close to stitching.

14. To gather ruffle strip, baste ⅛" from remaining long edge. Pull basting thread, gathering strip to fit bottom edge of yoke.

15. With wrong side of ruffle facing right side of bodice, baste ruffle along bottom edge of yoke, overlapping yoke ⅛". Stitching very close to gathered edge of ruffle, use a narrow width zigzag stitch with a short stitch length to stitch ruffle to yoke.

16. For yoke ruffle trim, cut an 11½" length of ⅜"w lace. Glue lace over gathered edge of ruffle.

17. For lace collar, cut a 5" length of 1"w lace. Matching wrong sides, press lace in half lengthwise. Insert neck edge between long edges of lace. Stitching close to long edges of lace, sew lace to bodice.

18. For skirt, cut a 6½" x 35" piece from dress fabric. For skirt ruffle, cut a 5" x 58" piece from fabric (pieced as necessary).

19. Matching right sides and short edges, refer to Fig. 2 to sew short edges of skirt piece together, leaving 2" unsewn at top of skirt (for back opening). Press seam open.

Fig. 2

2"

DOLL DRESS   (Continued)

20. For skirt ruffle, match right sides and short edges and sew short edges together. Press seam open. Matching wrong sides and raw edges, press fabric in half.

21. To gather ruffle, baste $\frac{1}{4}$″ and $\frac{1}{8}$″ from raw edge. Pull basting threads, gathering ruffle to fit bottom of skirt. Matching right sides and raw edges, sew ruffle to skirt. Press seam allowance toward skirt.

22. To attach skirt to bodice, baste $\frac{1}{4}$″ and $\frac{1}{8}$″ from top edge of skirt. Pull basting threads, gathering top of skirt to fit bottom of bodice. Matching right sides and raw edges, sew skirt to bodice. Turn right side out and press.

23. Press raw edges of back opening (including yoke ruffle) $\frac{1}{4}$″ to wrong side and stitch in place.

24. Remove any visible basting threads. Place dress on doll, overlapping opening edges. Mark placement for snaps. Remove dress from doll and sew on snaps.

25. Place dress on doll. Glue cameo button to dress. Tie ribbon for sash into a bow around waist; trim ends. Tuck flowers behind bow.

A SEAMSTRESS' WREATH   (Shown on page 30)

A 16″ square vine wreath provides the base for this collection of sewing memorabilia. We made a ribbon garland for our wreath by gluing an antique tape measure to the center of a $1\frac{2}{3}$ yd length of $1\frac{1}{2}$″w silk wired ribbon. The garland was loosely wound around the wreath and glued in place. We found our tape measure and all our other collectible sewing items at antique shops, but you can use treasured notions from your own collection to give your wreath a personal touch.

Dried roses, silk ivy, and sewing notions such as spools, button cards, thimbles, buttons, a sewing machine oil can, a button hook, a crochet hook, and a needle case were tucked among the vines of the wreath and glued in place.

Floral motifs cut from fabric which was stiffened with fusible interfacing were also glued to our wreath. Buttons were glued to the centers of some of the flowers.

The wreath makes a perfect frame for a collage of vintage sewing patterns. The envelopes and instructions were glued to a piece of cardboard which was then glued to the back of the wreath.

YOKE BACK
(cut 2, 1 in reverse)

BODICE BACK
(cut 2, 1 in reverse)

SLEEVE
(cut 2)

YOKE FRONT
(cut 1)

BODICE FRONT
(cut 1)

NEEDLEWORK CARRIER (Shown on page 29)

You will need 4 approx. 13½" x 19" reversible quilted fabric place mats with binding (we used octagonal place mats, but rectangular place mats will work as well), a 9" x 40" piece of 8-gauge clear vinyl (available at fabric stores), ½ yd of ⅜"w satin ribbon, thread to match place mats, assorted buttons and trims (we used lace trims, ribbons, a Battenberg lace doily, floral motifs cut from fabric, a heart cut from an old quilt, a gold charm, and a lace appliqué), seam ripper, fabric glue, and tracing paper.

Note: The Diagram, page 45, shows inside of completed carrier. Refer to Diagram to assemble carrier.

1. (*Note:* Follow Steps 1 - 5 for each side flap of carrier.) For side flap (A), refer to Fig. 1 and cut a 12½" piece from 1 place mat. Use seam ripper to remove binding from remainder of place mat; set binding aside and discard remainder of place mat.

Fig. 1

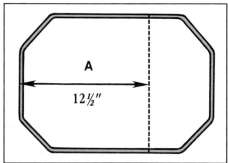

2. For vinyl pocket (B), refer to Fig. 2 and measure side flap from top to bottom. Cut a piece of vinyl 7½" wide by the determined measurement.

Fig. 2

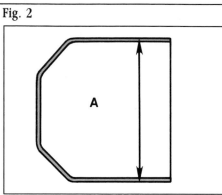

3. (*Note:* To sew vinyl, use tracing paper on both sides of seam to prevent presser foot from dragging; tear away paper after sewing.) To bind 1 long edge of vinyl for pocket opening, cut a piece of binding to fit 1 long edge of vinyl piece; insert long edge between folded edges of binding. Stitch binding to vinyl along previous stitching line.

4. Refer to Fig. 3 and remove stitching from 8½" of binding along top and bottom edges of side flap. Matching unbound edges of vinyl piece to raw edges of side flap, place vinyl on flap. Insert edges of vinyl and flap between folded edges of binding; restitch binding along previous stitching line.

Fig. 3

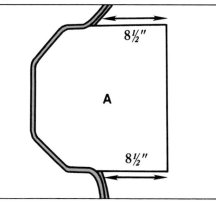

5. For pocket flap (C), refer to Fig. 4 and press left edge of side flap 3¾" toward pocket; topstitch ¼" from pressed edge.

Fig. 4

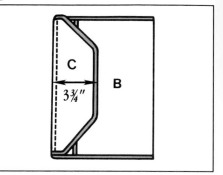

6. For center section (D), refer to Fig. 5 and cut a 10½"w piece from center of third place mat. Remove binding from end pieces; set binding aside and discard end pieces.

Fig. 5

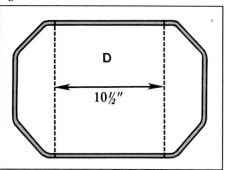

7. For large pocket on center section (E), refer to Fig. 6, page 45, and cut an 8¾" x 10½" piece from 1 end of remaining place mat. Remove binding from remainder of place mat; set binding aside and discard remainder of place mat.

Fig. 6

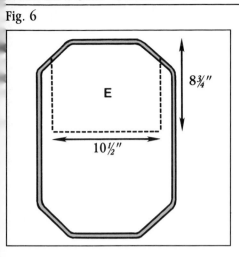

8. For small pockets on center section (F), cut a 5" x 10½" piece of vinyl. Repeat Step 3, page 44, to bind 1 long edge (top) of vinyl piece.
9. Matching side and bottom edges, place vinyl piece on large pocket. Referring to Fig. 7, topstitch through all layers 3" from left edge and ¼" from bottom edge of vinyl piece.

Fig. 7

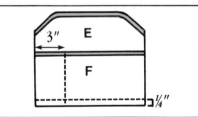

10. To attach pockets to center section, remove binding from 1 short edge (bottom) of center section. Matching bottom edges, place pockets right side up on center section. Insert bottom edge of pockets and center section between folded edges of binding; stitch binding along previous stitching line.
11. Measure 1 raw edge of center section; add ½". Cut 2 lengths of binding the determined measurement.

Open ends of each binding length and press ¼" to wrong side. Refold binding.
12. (*Note:* Refer to photo for remaining steps. Follow Step 12 to attach each side flap to center section.) Place 1 side flap on center section with pockets facing and raw edge of flap matching 1 raw edge of center section. Insert raw edges of flap and center section between long folded edges of 1 length of binding; stitch binding to carrier along previous stitching line.

13. For ties, cut ⅜"w ribbon in half. Press 1 end of each length ½" to 1 side. With carrier open, whipstitch pressed end of 1 tie to center left edge of left flap. With carrier closed, whipstitch pressed end of remaining tie to front of right flap opposite left tie.
14. Glue buttons and trims to left flap, trimming laces and ribbons to fit. Allow to dry.

DIAGRAM

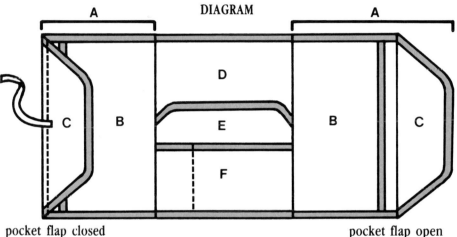

pocket flap closed   pocket flap open

GRANDMA'S SEWING DRAWER   (Shown on page 33)

For our nostalgic shadow box, we filled a drawer from an antique sewing machine cabinet with a collection of vintage sewing notions. We found our notions at antique shops, but you may have heirlooms or simple remembrances in your own sewing room with which to create your shadow box.

We lined our drawer with a piece of coarse ticking, cutting and pressing the fabric to fit and gluing it in place, and then turned the drawer on its side.

Then we arranged thread spools, needle and button cards, buttons, a pincushion, a sewing machine presser

foot, and a tape measure in the shadow box. These items can be glued in place, if desired.

Fusible interfacing was used to stiffen a piece of fabric from which we cut floral motifs. We glued buttons to the centers of some of the motifs. Arranging silk ivy leaves among the motifs, we glued both around the front edges of our shadow box.

A bow was tied from lengths of 1½"w organdy and silk wired ribbons and glued to the top of our shadow box, providing an elegant finishing touch.

Chart, page 56

Gentle Pastime

Long a favored pastime of gentlewomen,
flower gardening inspires a special feeling of
closeness to nature. Today, like those who came
before us, we delight in watching our gardens
flourish as we lovingly coax life from the
soil and nurture each tiny bud into bloom.
With the changing of the seasons comes new
beauty to please the senses — the soft petals of
spring, the lush greenery and fragrances
of summer, the rich hues of autumn, and the
bright berries of winter. Inspired by Paula's
Gentle Pastime, the projects in this collection are
designed to add pleasure to your moments
in the garden and to help you bring the
joys of nature indoors.

Painted Pot of Flowers, page 65

48

ℛecreating the lovely blossoms in Paula's painting, our bright bouquet brings the beauty of the garden into your home. A child's garden cart, discovered at an antique shop, provides a nostalgic spot to display the pot of flowers.

Decoupaged Garden Accessories, page 61
Garden Statue, page 65

𝒜n inexpensive plaster cherub is given the look of a costly lead garden statue using an easy painting technique. Decorated with colorful seed packets, a sponge-painted flower bucket holds a vibrant spray of fresh flowers.

$\mathcal{L}$ush green ivy is a perennial favorite among gardeners. Adding a touch of charm, it twines about a two-story birdhouse, creating a cheerful haven for a pair of little birds. A box stenciled with ivy keeps gardening tools, decorated flowerpots, and pretty gardening gloves close at hand. Perfect for puttering in the garden, a pair of overalls features a painted bird nest and trailing ivy.

Ivy-Covered Birdhouse, page 65
Potting Set, page 62

Bird Nest Overalls, page 63

rimmed with a white picket fence and summery flowers, a painted clock proclaims that it's always "time to garden." A vintage straw hat looks as if it could be home to a spring robin when adorned with ribbon, flowers, and a tiny bird nest.

Hat with Bird Nest, page 61

Seed Packet Sweatshirt, page 61

54

Like tiny works of art, colorful flower seed packets lend themselves beautifully to embellishing everyday items. An ordinary sweatshirt becomes high fashion when dressed up with color photocopies using an easy transfer technique. The decoupaged watering can makes tending your flowers a pleasure.

Decoupaged Garden Accessories, page 61

GENTLE PASTIME   (Shown on page 46)

X	DMC	¼X	B'ST	COLOR		X	DMC	¼X	½X	B'ST	COLOR		X	DMC	¼X	B'ST	COLOR
	blanc			white		✕	453				lt pearl grey		−	743			yellow
−	ecru			ecru		▲	500				dk blue green		2	744			lt yellow
	209			lt violet			501				blue green		★	801			lt brown
2	211			vy lt violet			502				lt blue green		✕	822			vy lt beige grey
	300			dk rust		□	503				vy lt blue green			838			vy dk beige brown
	317			steel grey			552				dk violet			839			dk beige brown
◇	368			lt green		★	553				violet		+	840			beige brown
□	400			rust		◉	640				dk beige grey			841			lt beige brown
	413		*	dk steel grey		◎	642				beige grey		☆	842			vy lt beige brown
✳	433		†	dk tan		▽	644				lt beige grey			844			dk grey
	434			tan		■	645				grey			890			vy dk green
△	435			lt tan		△	647				lt grey		▲	898			brown
◇	436			vy lt tan		+	648				vy lt grey			918			vy dk orange
	451			dk pearl grey			720				orange			920			dk orange
▽	452			pearl grey		4	741				dk yellow		◎	921			lt orange

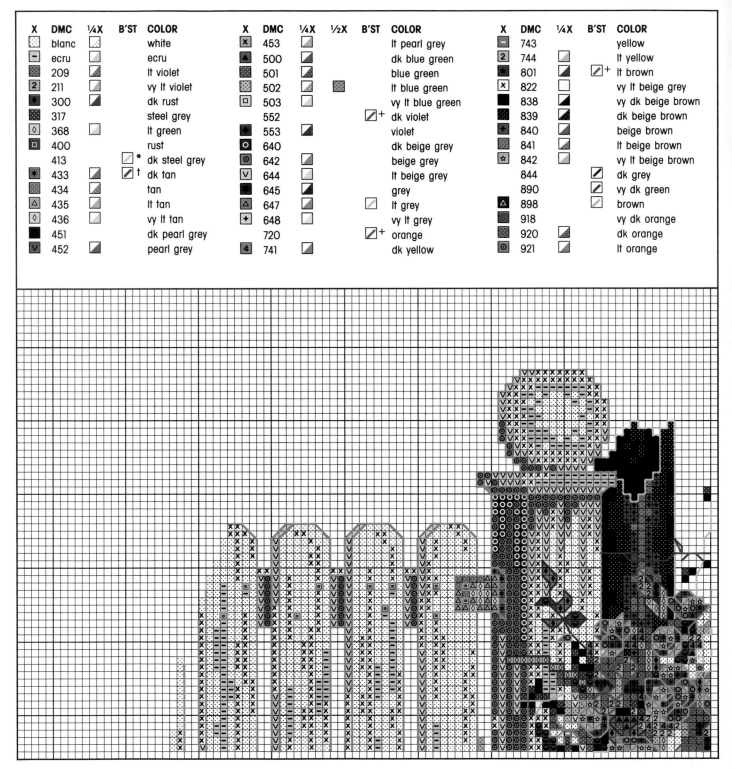

56

X	DMC	¼X	½X	B'ST	COLOR	X	DMC	¼X	½X	B'ST	COLOR
+	922	▨			vy lt orange	■	3685	◪		◪†	vy dk rose
★	930				dk blue	◉	3687				dk rose
◎	931				blue	▦	3688	◪			rose
−	932	▨			lt blue		3750			◪†	vy dk blue
	938			◪★	dk brown	★	3790	◪		◪	vy dk beige grey
✳	961	▨			dk pink	▨	Pink area indicates last row of previous section of design.				
☆	963	▨			lt pink						
◎	3013		▨		lt yellow green						
■	3031			◪★	vy dk brown	*	Dk steel grey for watering can and trowel. Vy dk brown for all other.				
▣	3033				beige						
☆	3072	▨			vy lt steel grey	†	Dk tan for barbed wire. Vy dk rose for violets. Vy dk blue for all other.				
◎	3326	▨			pink						
	3350			◪★	vy dk pink	+	Dk violet for irises. Orange for daisies. Lt brown for all other.				
◉	3363	▨		◪	dk yellow green						
◆	3364	▨			yellow green	★	Vy dk pink for roses and design on wheelbarrow. Dk brown for all other.				

GENTLE PASTIME (170w x 144h)			
14 count	12¼"	x	10⅜"
16 count	10⅝"	x	9"
18 count	9½"	x	8"
22 count	7¾"	x	6⅝"

Gentle Pastime (170w x 144h) was stitched over 2 fabric threads on a 22" x 20" piece of Cream Belfast Linen (32 ct). Two strands of floss were used for Cross Stitch and 1 for all other stitches. The design was custom framed.

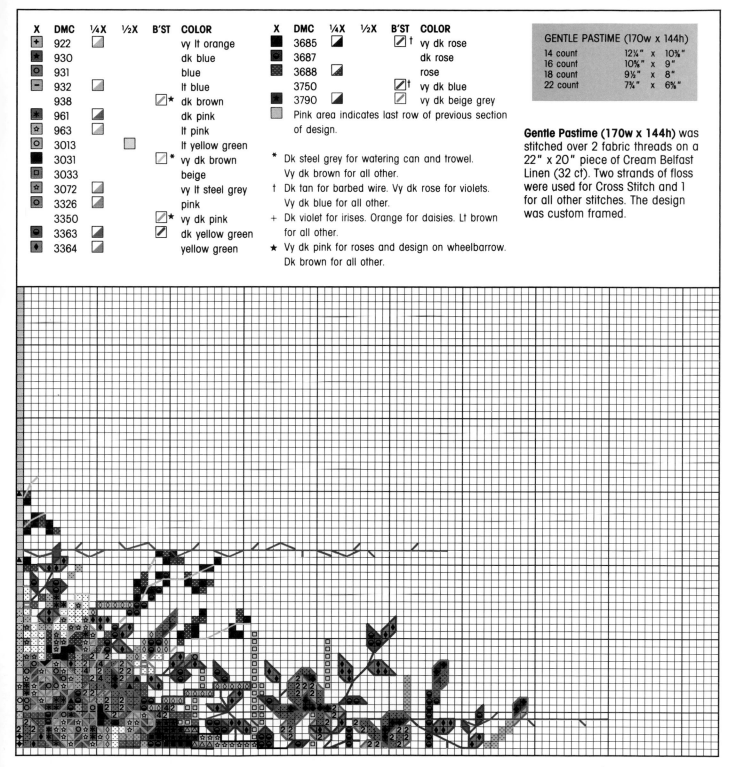

Continued on pages 58 and 59

"TIME TO GARDEN" CLOCK (Shown on page 52)

You will need a 6½"w x 10"h x 2¼"d unfinished wooden clock (we used a carriage clock from Walnut Hollow Farm®); battery-operated clock movement kit and clock hands; fine sandpaper; tack cloth; white, cream, vy lt blue, lt blue, lt blue green, blue green, yellow green, and brown acrylic paint; large flat paintbrushes; small round paintbrush; stencil brushes; paper towels; brown and black permanent felt-tip pens with fine points; matte waterbase varnish; tracing paper; removable tape; eleven ⅜"w wooden craft sticks; craft knife; hot glue gun; glue sticks; and small silk and preserved flowers and greenery (we used mini silk roses and daisies, purple silk wildflowers, and plumosa fern).

Note: Refer to photo for all steps. Allow to dry after each paint step unless otherwise indicated.

1. Sand clock; wipe lightly with tack cloth to remove dust.
2. For basecoat, paint clock cream. Paint top and feet of clock lt blue green.
3. For sky, use a large flat paintbrush to paint top ⅔ of front of clock vy lt blue. Before paint dries, dip a stencil brush in white paint and remove excess paint on paper towel (brush should be almost dry). Lightly stamp white paint unevenly over vy lt blue paint. Using a clean stencil brush for each color, repeat to stamp cream and lt blue paint over vy lt blue paint.
4. Trace face pattern onto tracing paper. To transfer pattern to clock, use a pencil to draw over lines of pattern on back of tracing paper. Position pattern pencil side down (right side up) on clock; tape to secure. Use a penny or the back of a spoon to rub over pattern. Remove pattern.

5. Use black pen to draw over transferred lines.
6. Mix 1 part yellow green paint and 1 part water. Use small round paintbrush to paint leaves and numbers on clock face.
7. For painted greenery behind fence and flowers, dip a large flat paintbrush into blue green paint and remove excess paint on paper towel (brush should be almost dry). Working from bottom to top and using long vertical strokes, lightly apply paint to front of clock below and around sides of clock face. Before paint dries, use a clean brush and repeat to apply yellow green paint over blue green paint.
8. For pickets in fence, use craft knife to trim 9 craft sticks to 3½".
9. Paint pickets and remaining craft sticks (rails) brown and then cream.
10. Lightly sand pickets and rails so that brown paint shows through in places. Wipe lightly with tack cloth to remove dust.
11. With bottom ends (square ends) even, place pickets ⅛" apart on a flat surface. Glue rails to pickets ½" and 2½" from tops of pickets. Turn fence over and use brown pen to draw nails on fence.
12. Use large flat paintbrush to apply varnish to clock and fence; allow to dry.
13. Glue greenery and flowers to clock.
14. Pulling some greenery and flowers through fence, place fence on clock in front of greenery and flowers; glue in place.
15. Follow manufacturer's instructions to assemble and attach clock movement and hands to clock.

60

HAT WITH BIRD NEST

(Shown on page 53)

For a quaint arrangement that brings the wonder of a backyard garden indoors, we decorated an antique hat with a sweet little bird nest and some colorful silk spring flowers.

We began by hot gluing a length of green grosgrain ribbon around the crown of an old straw hat we found at an antique shop. We then tied a bow from the same ribbon and glued it at the back of the hat.

The charming arrangement of silk lilac, mini roses, and dried munni grass has at its center a tiny nest with one egg intact and just the shell of another (the nest and eggs were purchased at a craft store). The nest and flowers were hot glued to the brim of the hat.

DECOUPAGED GARDEN ACCESSORIES

(Shown on pages 49 and 55)

You will need desired item to decoupage (we used a metal watering can and French flower bucket), dk blue green acrylic paint, a small piece of sponge, flower pictures cut from seed packets, matte Mod Podge® sealer, and a foam brush.

1. (*Note:* Refer to photos for all steps.) To paint item, wet sponge piece and wring out excess water. Using a light stamping motion, use sponge piece to paint sides of item dk blue green. Allow to dry.
2. Arrange flower pictures on sides of item, overlapping and trimming pictures to fit. Use sealer to glue pictures to item. Allow to dry.
3. Allowing to dry between coats, apply 2 coats of sealer to sides of item.

SEED PACKET SWEATSHIRT   (Shown on page 54)

Note: This project uses a photocopy transfer technique that requires the use of reverse image color photocopies. Most photocopy shops offer this service.

You will need a light-colored sweatshirt, reverse image color photocopies of seed packets, Sloman's® Stitchless Fabric Glue and Transfer Medium, foam brush, waxed paper, brayer or rolling pin, silk ivy, green dimensional fabric paint in squeeze bottle, removable fabric marking pen, and T-shirt form or cardboard covered with waxed paper.

1. Wash, dry, and press shirt according to glue and paint manufacturers' recommendations. Place T-shirt form in shirt. Test washability of ivy leaves by washing 1 leaf. Do not use leaves whose colors bleed.
2. Trim photocopies to desired size. Referring to photo, arrange photocopies on shirt. Use fabric marking pen to mark placement of photocopies. Turn photocopies image side down on shirt and trim as necessary to avoid overlapping.
3. For each transfer, use foam brush to apply an even coat of glue to front of photocopy so that image barely shows through glue. Without touching glue, place photocopy, glue side down, on shirt.
4. Cover photocopies with waxed paper. Firmly roll brayer over copies to remove any air bubbles. Remove waxed paper and allow glue to dry for 24 hours.
5. Remove T-shirt form. Heat-set transfers using a pressing cloth and a hot dry iron.

6. To remove paper from each transfer, brush a liberal amount of warm water over transfer; allow water to stand several minutes. Working from center to outside edges, use fingers to gently roll a thin layer of paper away from transfer (transfer will appear cloudy). Adding water as necessary, repeat process until transfer is as clear as original photocopy. Allow to dry.
7. To seal transfers, place T-shirt form in shirt. Mix 1 part glue and 1 part water. Apply a thin coat of glue mixture over each transfer. Allow to dry.
8. Remove ivy leaves from vines, discarding any plastic or metal pieces. Use a warm dry iron to press leaves flat.
9. For ivy vines, refer to photo and use fabric marking pen to draw desired vines on shirt.
10. For each leaf, use foam brush to apply glue to back of leaf. Place leaf glue side down on shirt.
11. Cover leaves with waxed paper. Firmly roll brayer over leaves to remove any air bubbles. Remove waxed paper and allow glue to dry.
12. Use green paint to paint over pen lines for vines. Allow to dry.
13. To launder, follow glue and paint manufacturers' recommendations.

For each pot, you will need a terra-cotta pot, flower motif(s) cut from wrapping paper or seed packets, dk yellow green and cream acrylic paint, foam brushes, matte Mod Podge® sealer, small piece of sponge, tracing paper (optional), and natural-colored raffia.

For gloves, you will need light-colored fabric garden gloves, 1 yd of ⅟₁₆"w green satin ribbon, and a large needle.

For box, you will need matte clear acrylic spray and either desired painted wooden box or the following items: an unfinished wooden box, medium sandpaper, tack cloth, cream acrylic paint, lt brown waterbase stain, foam brushes, and a soft cloth.

For gloves and box, you will also need acetate for stencils (available at craft or art supply stores), stencil brush, paper towels, craft knife, cutting mat or a thick layer of newspapers, green acrylic paint, green permanent felt-tip pen with fine point, and removable tape (optional).

POT

1. (*Note:* Refer to photo for all steps.) Wet sponge piece and wring out excess water. Using a light stamping motion, use sponge piece to paint sides of pot below rim dk yellow green. Allow to dry.

2. Use foam brush to paint rim of pot cream. Allow to dry.

3. If painted oval is desired, trace oval pattern onto tracing paper; cut out. Place pattern in desired position on pot and use a pencil to lightly draw around pattern. Paint oval cream; allow to dry.

4. Use sealer to glue flower motif(s) to rim or painted oval. Allow to dry.

5. Allowing to dry between coats, apply 2 coats of sealer to outside of pot.

6. Tie several lengths of raffia into a bow around pot.

GLOVES

1. (*Note:* Refer to photo for all steps.) Use ivy leaf patterns, page 63, and green paint and follow Stenciling, page 124, to stencil desired leaves on gloves.

2. Use green pen to draw veins, vines, and tendrils on and around leaves.

3. For ribbon trim, cut ribbon in half. Thread needle with 1 ribbon length. Beginning and ending at center front of 1 glove, use a Running Stitch, page 125, to stitch on cuff approx. ⅜" from seam. Tie ribbon ends into a bow. Repeat for remaining glove.

BOX

1. (*Note:* If a finished box is used, begin with Step 4. Refer to photo for all steps.) Paint box cream. Allow to dry.

2. Sand box, removing paint in places. Wipe lightly with tack cloth to remove dust.

3. Use a damp foam brush to apply stain to box; use soft cloth to wipe off excess. Allow to dry.

4. Use ivy leaf patterns, page 63, and green paint and follow Stenciling, page 124, to stencil desired leaves on box.

5. Use green pen to draw veins, vines, and tendrils on and around leaves.

6. Allowing to dry between coats, apply 2 coats of acrylic spray to box.

BIRD NEST OVERALLS (Shown on page 51)

You will need a pair of light-colored overalls; green, brown, dk brown, and lt grey fabric paint; small flat fabric paintbrushes; green and brown permanent felt-tip pens with fine points; brown and dk brown permanent felt-tip pens with medium points; stencil brush; paper towels; acetate for stencils (available at craft or art supply stores); craft knife; cutting mat or a thick layer of newspapers; removable tape; tracing paper; and a T-shirt form or cardboard covered with waxed paper.

1. Wash, dry, and press overalls according to paint manufacturer's recommendations. Place T-shirt form in overalls.
2. (*Note:* Refer to photo for remaining steps.) Trace bird nest and branch patterns, page 64, onto separate pieces of tracing paper; do not cut out. Position patterns on bib of overalls, adjusting placement of branch patterns to fit bib; tape patterns together to form 1 pattern.
3. To transfer pattern to bib, use a pencil to draw over lines of pattern on back of tracing paper. Position pattern pencil side down (right side up) on bib; tape to secure. Use a penny or the back of a spoon to rub over pattern. Remove pattern.

4. Use water to dilute lt grey, brown, and dk brown paint to a watercolor consistency.
5. Use a fabric paintbrush to paint eggs with diluted lt grey paint, leaving part of each egg unpainted for highlight. Allow to dry.
6. Paint branches with diluted brown paint, leaving parts of branches unpainted for highlights. While brown paint is still wet, shade branches with diluted dk brown paint, allowing colors to blend together. Allow to dry.
7. Use brown pen with fine point to draw over all transferred lines. Use dk brown pen with medium point to color inside of nest around eggs. Use brown and dk brown pens with medium points to draw lines on outside of nest to resemble twigs.
8. Use ivy leaf patterns and green paint and follow Stenciling, page 124, to stencil desired leaves on bird nest, along top and side edges of bib, and along pockets.
9. Use green pen to draw veins, vines, and tendrils on and around leaves.
10. Remove T-shirt form. If necessary, heat-set designs according to paint manufacturer's recommendations.
11. To launder overalls, follow paint manufacturer's recommendations.

IVY LEAVES

Patterns continued on page 64

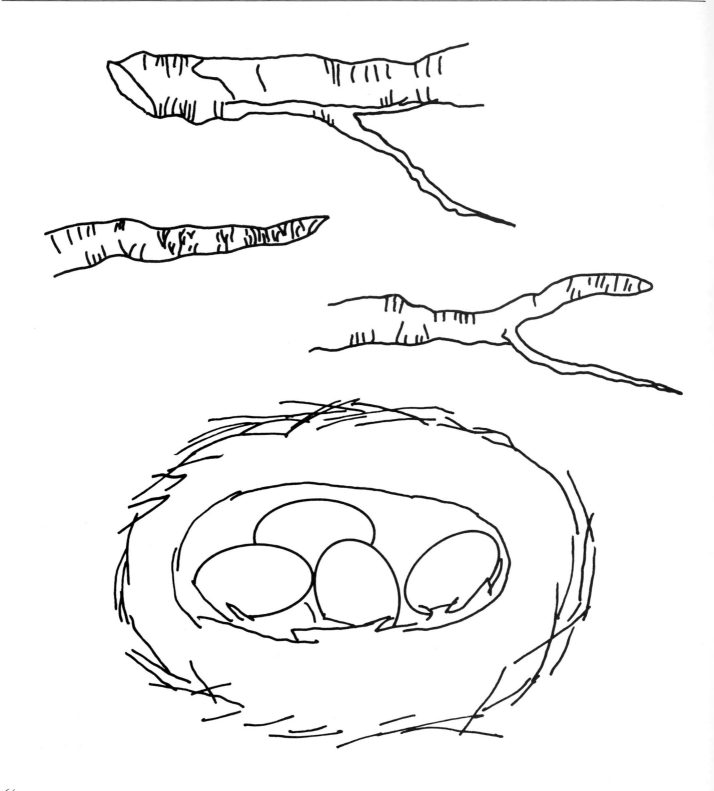

IVY-COVERED BIRDHOUSE
(Shown on page 50)

You will need an unfinished wooden birdhouse (we used a two-story 4¾"w x 11"h x 4"d birdhouse); white, yellow green, and dk yellow green acrylic paint; brown waterbase stain; foam brushes; a soft cloth; stencil brushes; paper towels; acetate for stencils (available at craft or art supply stores); craft knife; cutting mat or a thick layer of newspapers; removable tape (optional); green permanent felt-tip pen with fine point; fine sandpaper; tack cloth; small twigs; silk ivy; 2 artificial birds; hot glue gun; glue sticks; and matte clear acrylic spray.

1. Sand birdhouse. Wipe lightly with tack cloth to remove dust.
2. (*Note:* Refer to photo for remaining steps. Allow to dry after each paint color.) Paint walls of birdhouse white. Paint roof, base, and any trim dk yellow green.
3. Use ivy leaf patterns, page 63, and yellow green paint and follow Stenciling, page 124, to stencil desired leaves on birdhouse, shading leaves with dk yellow green.
4. Use green pen to draw veins, vines, and tendrils on and around leaves.
5. Use damp foam brush to apply stain to birdhouse; remove excess with soft cloth. Allow to dry.
6. Allowing to dry between coats, apply 2 coats of acrylic spray to birdhouse.
7. Glue twigs and ivy to roof. Glue birds to birdhouse.

PAINTED POT OF FLOWERS
(Shown on page 48)

A child's garden cart that was an exciting find at an antique auction provides the perfect spot for our painted flowerpot, which features an arrangement of silk "fresh-from-the-garden" flowers.

For an old-fashioned container to hold our floral gathering, we painted a large terra-cotta flowerpot, giving it a weathered appearance. Using a damp sponge piece, we lightly sponged dk brown acrylic paint over the entire pot. Using a fresh sponge piece for each color and allowing the paint to dry between colors, we then sponged brown, lt brown, beige, cream, and white paint unevenly over the pot. Finally, we used a small round paintbrush to paint brown lines on the pot to resemble cracks. Two coats of matte clear acrylic spray protect the painted finish.

The flowers in the pot were arranged in a block of floral foam that was placed in the pot and covered with green Spanish moss. A garden of silk bulb flowers and perennials were included. Full-blown pink roses and showy purple irises compete for attention with daisies, mums, and marigolds. Wild berry sprays and purple, pink, and yellow wildflowers add to the splendid riot of color.

GARDEN STATUE
(Shown on page 49)

Note: Statue is suitable for protected outdoor use, but should not be exposed to weather.

You will need a plaster statue, lt tan and charcoal grey acrylic paint, foam brushes, disposable cups, a disposable pie tin, a bottle or can to support statue during painting, and matte clear acrylic spray.

1. Place bottle or can in pie tin; place statue on bottle or can.
2. For basecoat, use a foam brush to paint statue lt tan. Allow to dry.
3. For second coat, mix 1 part grey paint and 1 part water in a cup; set aside. For topcoat, mix 1 part lt tan paint, 1 part grey paint, and 2 parts water in another cup; set aside.
4. (*Note:* Refer to photo for remaining steps.) To apply second coat, slowly pour paint mixture over top of statue, covering entire surface of statue. Use foam brush, if necessary, to fill any unpainted crevices with paint.
5. While second coat is still wet, slowly pour topcoat mixture over top of statue, allowing paint to streak and run. Allow to dry.
6. Allowing to dry between coats, apply 2 coats of acrylic spray to statue.

Delicate Beauties

Whether spilling from a pretty vase or winding about a trellis in the garden, old-fashioned roses have an age-old appeal. Their fullness and soft colors touch our lives with gentle beauty and inspire a romantic mood. Paula Vaughan captures this nostalgic feeling in her Delicate Beauties, which returns us to a time when genteel ladies took pleasure in tending lush rose gardens and pursuing their favorite needlecrafts. Like these women of generations past, we too delight in the matchless allure and fragrance of this queen of flowers.

Chart, page 74

avored pastimes from yesteryear continue to bring pleasure to our lives today. Adapting the handicraft of quilting to modern fashion, a feminine jacket made by strip-quilting onto a men's shirt is nice for cool days. Reminiscent of the Victorians' love of birds, a whitewashed bird cage is adorned with a springtime bouquet to create a fanciful accent for the bedroom.

Strip-Quilted Jacket, page 82

A Lovebird's Cage, page 83

*T*he charm of roses adds a special enchantment to our homes. A tiny nosegay dresses up a decorative soap basket for the bath, and a cross-stitched bouquet graces a fabric-covered photograph album. Recreating the lovely Grandmother's Fan quilt in Paula's painting, a handmade quilt and matching pillow shams feature a quilted rose motif.

Rosy Bath Basket, page 83
Delicate Nosegay Photo Album, page 84

Grandmother's Fan Quilt, page 78
Grandmother's Fan Pillow Shams, page 81

Delicate Nosegay Sweater, page 84

*W*e can enjoy the beauty of roses all year long when we use our talents to preserve their graceful image. Capturing a delicate bouquet with needle and thread, a cross-stitched sweater makes a pretty addition to a lady's wardrobe. A beribboned wreath of roses and other florals brings a breath of spring to a door or wall.

Wreath of Roses, page 83

DELICATE BEAUTIES (Shown on page 67)

X	DMC	¼X	½X	B'ST	COLOR	X	DMC	¼X	½X	B'ST	COLOR	X	DMC	¼X	½X	B'ST	COLOR
	blanc				white		500			*	vy dk green		754				lt peach
	ecru				ecru		501				dk green		758				dk peach
	221				red		502				green		783			★	dk gold
	312			*	royal blue		503				lt green		801				vy dk brown
	319			†	dk yellow green		504				vy lt green		801			‡	vy dk brown
	335				dk rose		642				beige grey		819				lt pink
	353				peach		644				lt beige grey		822				vy lt beige
	368				yellow green		646			+	dk grey		841				beige brown
	372				khaki		647				grey		899				rose
	433			+	dk brown		648				lt grey		926				grey blue
	434			+	brown		676				gold		927				lt grey blue
	435				lt brown		677				lt gold		930				vy dk blue
	436				vy lt brown		743				yellow		931				dk blue
	437				tan		746				vy lt gold		932				blue

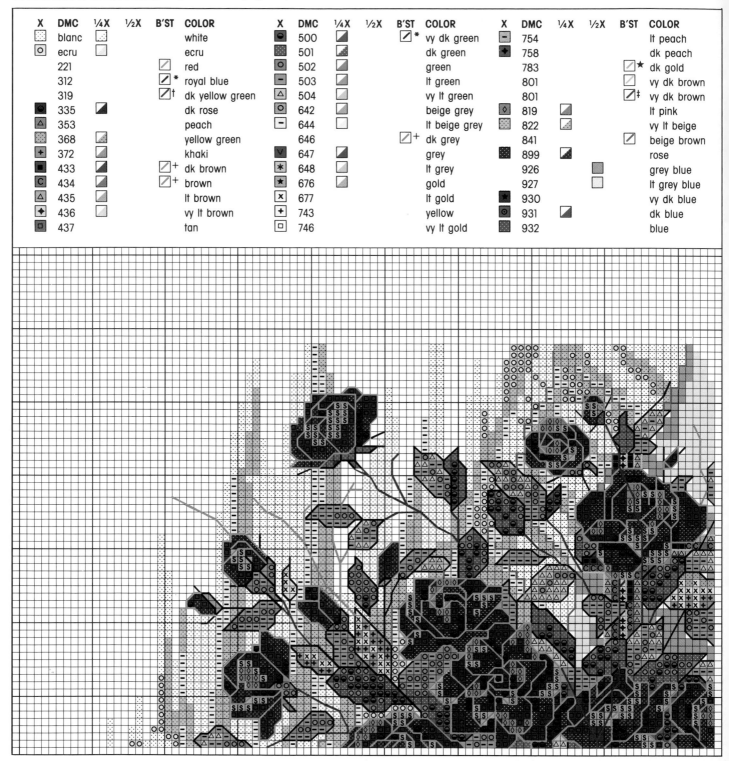

X	DMC	1/4X	1/2X	B'ST	COLOR	X	DMC	1/4X	1/2X	B'ST	COLOR
S	963	◪			vy lt rose	⊡	646	French Knot			dk grey
x	3013	◪			lt yellow green	⊘	646	Lazy Daisy			dk grey
▦	3032	◪			dk beige grey	▨					Grey area indicates last row of previous section of design.
C	3033	◪			lt beige						
✿	3041				dk violet						
⊙	3042				violet						
▪	3326	◪			lt rose						
	3350			◪*	vy dk rose						
-	3716				pink						
V	3743				lt violet						
△	3752				lt blue						
2	3753				vy lt blue						
▨	3782	◪	◪	◪†	beige						
✦	3790	◪			dk beige						

* Royal blue for quilt, thread on spool, and thread in needle in pincushion. Vy dk green for leaves. Vy dk rose for thread in needle in hoop.
† Beige for quilt. Use 3 strands of dk yellow green for stems.
+ Dk brown for twigs. Brown for spool. Dk grey for vase, needles, and pins.
★ Dk gold for quilt. Use 1 strand of dk gold and 1 strand of Kreinik Balger® Blending Filament #002HL gold·for vase.
‡ Use 3 strands of vy dk brown.

DELICATE BEAUTIES (176w x 144h)		
14 count	12⅝"	x 10⅜"
16 count	11"	x 9"
18 count	9⅞"	x 8"
22 count	8"	x 6⅝"

Delicate Beauties (176w x 144h) was stitched over 2 fabric threads on a 23" x 21" piece of Cream Belfast Linen (32 ct). Two strands of floss were used for Cross Stitch and 1 for all other stitches unless otherwise noted. The design was custom framed.

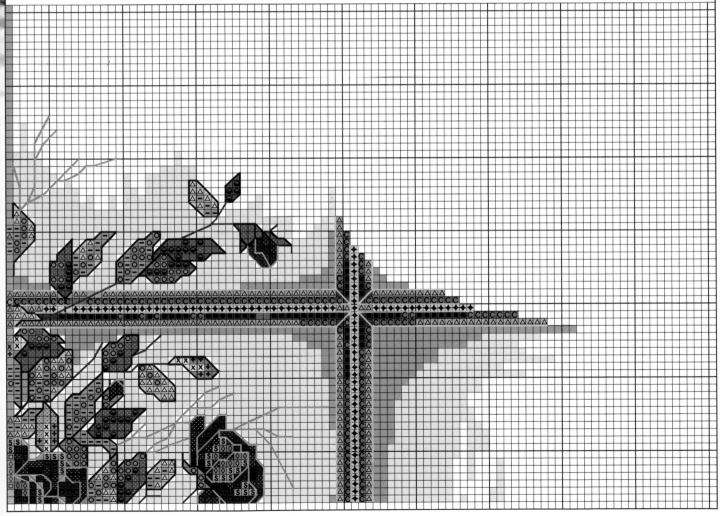

Continued on pages 76 and 77

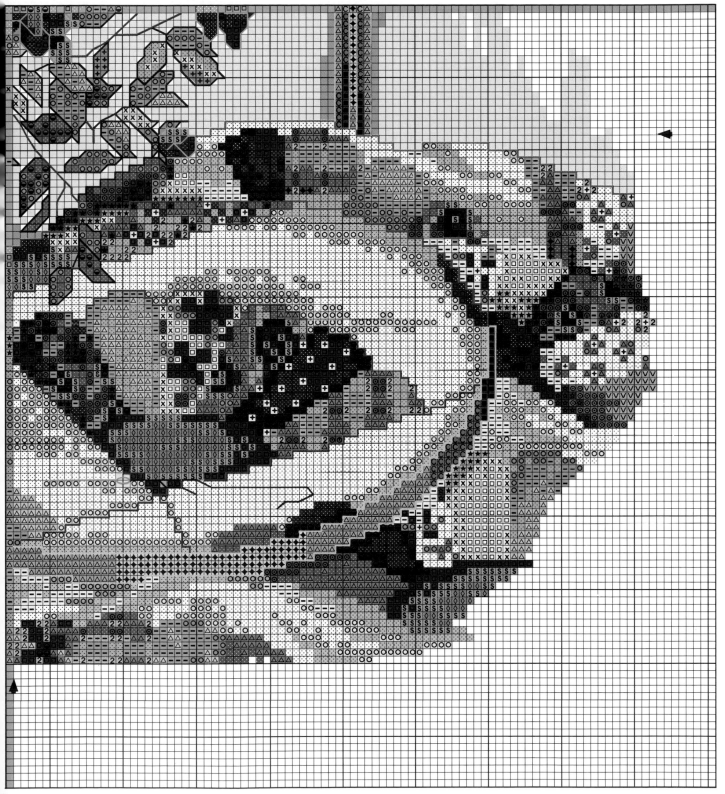

For a queen-size quilt (approx. 82" x 93"), you will need 6½ yds of 44"w unbleached muslin fabric for borders, background pieces, and binding; 2½ yds of 44"w cotton print fabric for borders and fan centers; coordinating cotton print fabrics for fan pieces (we used approx. 4½ yds *total* from 17 different 44"w print fabrics); 3 yds of 90"w unbleached muslin fabric for backing; a queen-size piece (90" x 108") of polyester bonded quilt batting; tracing paper; transparent tape; lightweight cardboard; silver colored or #2 lead pencil; white eraser; quilting hoop or frame; quilting needle; and off-white sewing thread and quilting thread.

Note: Refer to Diagram, page 79, to assemble quilt and mark quilting lines. Patterns include a ¼" seam allowance. For each sewing step, match right sides and raw edges and pin fabric pieces together; unless otherwise indicated, use a ¼" seam allowance to sew fabric pieces together. Clip curves and press seam allowances to 1 side (toward darker fabric where possible).

1. Wash and dry all fabrics. Trim selvages from fabrics and press.
2. For Pattern A (background piece), trace Patterns A1, A2, and A3, pages 80 and 81, onto tracing paper; cut out. Matching registration marks ($\oplus$), overlap patterns to form Pattern A; tape pieces together.
3. Trace Pattern B (fan center) and Pattern C (fan piece), page 79, onto tracing paper; cut out.
4. Use patterns and cut 1 cardboard template from each pattern; label templates. Do not discard Pattern A.

5. Use Template A and cut 42 background pieces from 44"w muslin fabric. Use Template B and cut 42 fan centers from print fabric. Use Template C and cut 336 fan pieces from coordinating print fabrics.
6. (*Note:* Follow Step 6 to make 42 quilt blocks.) For fan, choose 8 fan pieces. Sew 2 fan pieces together along 1 long edge. Repeat to attach remaining 6 pieces. Matching curved edge of 1 fan center to bottom curved edge of fan, sew fan center to fan, easing as necessary. Matching curved edge of 1 background piece to top curved edge of fan, sew background piece to fan, easing as necessary.
7. Sew quilt blocks together to form quilt top.
8. (*Note:* For Steps 8 - 10, piece border strips as necessary.) For inner muslin border, cut a 2½"w strip from 44"w muslin fabric the length of the right edge of quilt top; sew strip to right edge of quilt top. Cut a 2½"w muslin strip the width of the quilt top including added border; sew strip to bottom edge of quilt top.
9. For print border, cut two 2½"w print strips the width of the quilt top including added border; sew strips to top and bottom edges of quilt top. Cut two 2½"w print strips the length of the quilt top including added borders; sew strips to side edges of quilt top.
10. For outer muslin border, repeat Step 9, cutting 5¼"w muslin strips.
11. To mark quilting lines on quilt top, position Pattern A under quilt top and use silver or #2 pencil to lightly trace rose design onto each quilt block. Trace design at each corner of outer muslin border. Trace large rose and leaves only at center of top, bottom, and each side

of outer muslin border. Use a ruler to mark quilting lines at 1¼" intervals between designs on muslin border.
12. Place backing fabric wrong side up. Center batting on wrong side of backing. Center quilt top, right side up, on batting. Pin all layers together. Basting from center outward, baste layers together from corner to corner. With basting lines 3" to 4" apart, baste from top to bottom and from side to side. Baste close to edges.
13. Insert basted layers in hoop or frame. To quilt, use quilting thread and follow Quilting, page 126, working from the center of the quilt outward. Quilt ''in the ditch'' (close to seamlines) along all seams; quilt along all marked lines. Trim batting and backing even with quilt top. Erase any visible marked quilting lines.
14. To round corners of quilt, place curved edge of Template B over 1 corner of quilt. Draw around curved edge of pattern. Repeat for remaining corners. Cut along drawn lines.
15. For binding, cut one 2"w bias strip 10 yds long (pieced as necessary) from muslin fabric. Match wrong sides and raw edges and press bias strip in half lengthwise; press long raw edges to center.
16. Unfold 1 end of binding; press end ¼" to wrong side; refold. Unfold 1 long edge of binding. Beginning with pressed end, pin unfolded edge of binding along edge on front of quilt. Continue pinning binding around quilt until ends of binding overlap ½"; trim excess binding. Using pressed line closest to raw edge as a guide, sew binding to quilt. Fold binding over raw edges to back of quilt; whipstitch in place. Remove basting threads.

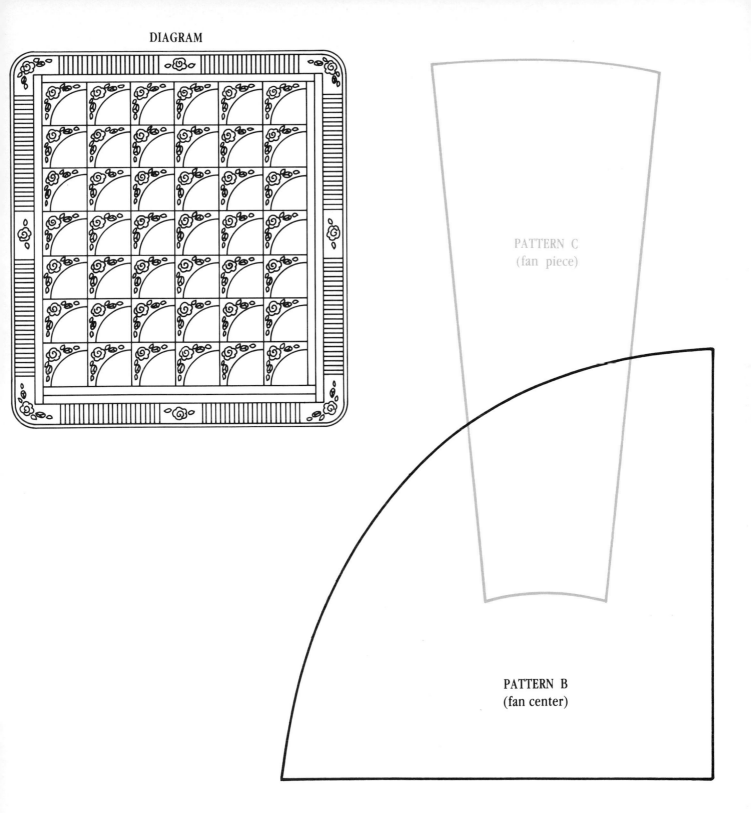

DIAGRAM

PATTERN C
(fan piece)

PATTERN B
(fan center)

Patterns continued on pages 80 and 81

PATTERN A1
(background piece)

GRANDMOTHER'S FAN PILLOW SHAMS   (Shown on page 71)

For each standard sham (approx. 26" x 37" including 3½"w ruffle), you will need 4 yds of 44"w unbleached muslin fabric for sham and ruffle, ½ yd of 44"w cotton print fabric for borders and fan centers, coordinating cotton print fabrics for fan pieces (we used approx. ½ yd *total* from 10 different 44"w print fabrics), one 24" x 36" piece of polyester bonded batting, tracing paper, transparent tape, lightweight cardboard, silver colored or #2 lead pencil, white eraser, quilting hoop or frame, quilting needle, and off-white sewing thread and quilting thread.

Note: Patterns include a ¼" seam allowance. For each sewing step, match right sides and raw edges and pin fabric pieces together; unless otherwise indicated, use a ¼" seam allowance to sew fabric pieces together. Clip curves and press seam allowances to 1 side (toward darker fabric where possible).

1. Follow Steps 1 - 4 of Grandmother's Fan Quilt instructions, page 78, to prepare fabrics, patterns, and templates.
2. Use Template A and cut 2 background pieces from muslin fabric. Use Template B and cut 2 fan centers from print fabric. Use Template C and cut 16 fan pieces from coordinating print fabrics.

3. (*Note:* Refer to photo for remaining steps.) Follow Step 6 of Grandmother's Fan Quilt instructions, page 78, to make 2 quilt blocks. Sew blocks together to form sham top.
4. For inner muslin border, cut a 2½"w muslin strip the width of the sham top; sew strip to bottom edge of sham top. Cut a 2½"w muslin strip the length of the sham top including added border; sew strip to right edge of sham top.
5. For print border, cut two 1¾"w print strips the length of the sham top including added border; sew strips to side edges of sham top. Cut two 1¾"w print strips the width of the sham top including added borders; sew strips to top and bottom edges of sham top.
6. For outer muslin border, repeat Step 5, cutting 2½"w muslin strips.
7. To mark quilting lines on sham top, position Pattern A under sham top and use silver or #2 pencil to lightly trace rose design onto each quilt block.
8. For sham top backing, cut a piece of muslin fabric same size as sham top.
9. To quilt sham top, follow Steps 12 and 13 of Grandmother's Fan Quilt instructions, page 78.
10. For sham back, cut two 13"w muslin pieces the width of the sham top.

Press 1 long edge of each back piece ½" to 1 side (wrong side); press ½" to wrong side again and stitch in place. With right sides up, overlap finished edges of back pieces 4" and baste together.
11. For ruffle, cut an 8"w muslin strip 6¼ yds long (pieced as necessary). Match right sides and short edges and use a ½" seam allowance to sew short edges together; press seam open. With wrong sides together, match raw edges and fold ruffle in half; press. Baste ½" and ¼" from raw edge. Pull basting threads, drawing up gathers to fit sham top.
12. Matching raw edges, baste ruffle to right side of sham top.
13. Place sham top and back right sides together. Using a ½" seam allowance, sew top and back together. Cut corners diagonally. Remove basting threads at opening; turn sham right side out. Remove remaining basting threads; press.

PATTERN A2
(background piece)

PATTERN A3
(background piece)

STRIP-QUILTED JACKET (Shown on page 68)

Note: This jacket is constructed using a men's shirt as a base. The shirt is taken apart, the pieces are quilted, and then the shirt is reassembled. The finished jacket will be approx. 2 sizes smaller than the original shirt. Choose shirt size accordingly.

You will need a long-sleeved cotton blend shirt (we used a men's XL oxford cloth shirt), coordinating cotton print fabrics for quilting strips and binding (we used 8 different print fabrics), fusible fleece, tracing paper, removable fabric marking pen, thread to match fabrics, and seam ripper.

1. Wash, dry, and press shirt and fabrics.

2. Place shirt on a flat surface and use fabric marking pen to draw a line across bottom of shirt at desired finished length. Cut off bottom of shirt along drawn line.

3. Use seam ripper to remove pockets, collar, cuffs, plackets, and any buttons and trim from shirt; discard or set aside for another use.

4. Use seam ripper to take shirt apart at side and sleeve seams, armhole seams, and shoulder seams. Baste sleeve plackets closed. Press shirt front, back, and sleeve pieces flat (including any tucks).

5. For strip patterns, measure length of longest shirt piece; add 3″. Use a ruler to draw 4 separate strip patterns on tracing paper the determined length by the following widths: 2½″, 2″, 1¾″, and 1½″ (piece tracing paper together with tape if necessary). Cut out patterns.

6. (*Note:* Follow Steps 6 - 13 for each shirt piece.) Matching right side of shirt piece to fusible side of fleece, draw around shirt piece on fleece. Cut out fleece piece ¼″ inside drawn line. Following manufacturer's instructions, center and fuse fleece piece to right side of shirt piece.

7. Place shirt piece, fleece side up, on a flat surface. Use fabric marking pen to draw a line down center of shirt piece from top to bottom.

8. Using desired width pattern, cut a strip from 1 quilting strip fabric. Using desired width pattern, cut a second strip from another fabric.

9. Center first strip right side up on shirt piece with 1 long edge along drawn line. Overlapping long edges of strips ½″ (for seam allowance), place second strip right side up on opposite side of marked line.

10. Alternating pattern widths and fabrics and overlapping long edges of strips ½″, cut strips to cover shirt piece. Do not trim strips even with edges of shirt piece at this time. To mark placement of strips, use fabric marking pen and number strips at 1 end.

11. Set aside all strips except the 2 strips next to the drawn line. Matching 1 long edge, place strips right sides together. Center matched long edge of strips along drawn line on shirt piece. Stitching through all layers, sew strips to shirt piece ¼″ from long edge (Fig. 1). Press strips open (right side out).

Fig. 1

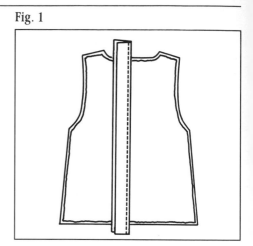

12. (*Note:* Sew strips to shirt piece in order determined in Step 10.) With right sides together, match 1 long edge of next strip to unsewn long edge of 1 sewn strip. Stitching through all layers, sew strip to shirt piece ¼″ from long edge. Press strip open (Fig. 2). Repeat to sew remaining strips to shirt piece.

Fig. 2

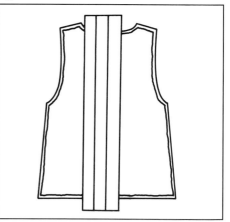

STRIP-QUILTED JACKET
(Continued)

13. Baste close to edges of shirt piece. Trim pieced strips even with edges of shirt piece.

14. (*Note:* When assembling jacket, baste or pin pieces together, try on jacket, and adjust fit if necessary before sewing; use seam allowance needed for proper fit.) Matching right sides and raw edges and easing as necessary, sew shirt pieces together in the following order: shoulder seams, armhole seams, and side and sleeve seams.

15. Try on jacket and trim sleeves to desired length if necessary.

16. For sleeve binding, measure around 1 sleeve opening; add 2". Cut two 2"w bias strips the determined measurement. For binding for remaining edges of jacket, measure around neckline, down 1 front opening from neckline to bottom of jacket, around bottom of jacket, and up remaining front opening; add 2". Cut one 2"w bias strip (pieced as necessary) the determined measurement.

17. Press ends of each bias strip ½" to wrong side. Matching wrong sides, press each strip in half lengthwise; press long edges to center.

18. To bind each sleeve, insert raw edge of sleeve between long folded edges of 1 bias strip, overlapping ends of strip; baste in place. Stitching close to inner edge of binding, sew binding to sleeve. Remove all visible basting threads.

19. To bind remaining edges of jacket, begin at center back of bottom of jacket and repeat Step 18, mitering binding at corners.

A LOVEBIRD'S CAGE (Shown on page 69)

An enchanting scene can be created when a decorative birdcage is topped with a lovely spray of silk, preserved, and dried flowers. To decorate our whitewashed wood-and-wire birdcage, we arranged silk tea roses, preserved yellow roses, and twigs into a luxurious bundle to fit the contours of the cage.

The larger flowers were enhanced by the addition of silk narcissus, tiny sweetheart rosebuds, and purple wildflowers, as well as dried blue hydrangea. The stems of all were wrapped together with florist tape, and the entire spray was hot glued to the birdcage.

A bow tied from 1½"w cream silk wired ribbon was hot glued near the stems of the bouquet. A second bow tied from satin and grosgrain ribbons in various colors and widths was hot glued atop the first bow. The ribbon streamers were arranged around and among the flowers.

A mischievous little artificial lovebird, seemingly just escaped, was perched safely among the flowers.

WREATH OF ROSES
(Shown on page 73)

For our romantic wreath, a variety of dried and preserved flowers were arranged and hot glued among the twigs of a 15" dia. elm wreath.

We began with dried white German statice, purple sinuata statice, and yellow alchemilla to provide a background of vivid contrasts for the larger flowers.

Preserved pink roses and dried yellow roses were then added to the wreath. These were complemented by dried helichrysum, globe amaranth, and hydrangea.

Preserved mini oak, salal leaves, and plumosa fern bring to our wreath the untamed air of an English garden.

Delicate bows tied from 2"w lengths of rose and green organdy ribbon were hot glued among the flowers to lend a subtle texture and help unify the garden of colors in this rich floral display.

ROSY BATH BASKET
(Shown on page 70)

Dried and preserved flowers transform a simple basket into a charming accent for the bath. We decorated our 7½" dia. whitewashed basket with two preserved yellow roses, one dried pink rose with greenery, and a touch of dried blue hydrangea. Arranged in a small bouquet together with some tiny twigs, the flowers and greenery were hot glued to the basket.

A bow tied from lengths of satin ribbon was hot glued among the flowers. The basket was lined with a dainty lace-trimmed handkerchief found at an antique shop.

DELICATE NOSEGAY SWEATER
(Shown on page 72)

You will need a sweater, 9″ square of 8.5 mesh waste canvas, embroidery floss (see color key, page 85), 9″ square of lightweight non-fusible interfacing, masking tape, embroidery hoop (optional), tweezers, sewing thread, and a spray bottle filled with water.

1. Cover edges of canvas with masking tape.
2. Referring to photo for placement of design, mark center of design on sweater with a pin.
3. Match center of canvas to pin. Use blue threads in canvas to place canvas straight on sweater; pin canvas to sweater. Pin interfacing to wrong side of sweater under canvas. Baste securely around edges of canvas through all 3 layers. Baste from corner to corner and from side to side.
4. (*Note:* Using a hoop is recommended when working on a sweater.) Work design on canvas, stitching from large holes to large holes. Use 6 strands of floss for Cross Stitch and 2 for Backstitch unless otherwise indicated.
5. Remove basting threads and trim canvas to within ¾″ of design. Spray canvas with water until it becomes limp. Using tweezers, pull out canvas threads 1 at a time.
6. Trim interfacing close to design.

DELICATE NOSEGAY PHOTO ALBUM (Shown on page 70)

You will need a 10″ square of Cream Belfast Linen (32 ct), embroidery floss (see color key, page 85), photo album that measures at least 7″ x 8″ (we used an 8½″ x 9½″ album), fabric to cover album (see Step 8 for amount), ½ yd each of 1″w pregathered lace and ³⁄₁₆″ dia. twisted satin cord to match fabric, medium weight cardboard, polyester bonded batting, fabric glue, and tracing paper.

1. Follow Working On Linen, page 125, to work design over 2 threads on linen. Use 2 strands of floss for Cross Stitch and 1 for Backstitch unless otherwise indicated.
2. Trace oval pattern onto tracing paper; cut out.
3. Place stitched piece wrong side up on a flat surface. Center oval pattern over stitched design and use a pencil to lightly draw around pattern. Cutting ½″ outside pencil line, cut out stitched piece.
4. Use oval pattern and cut 1 oval from cardboard and 2 ovals from batting.
5. (*Note:* Allow to dry after each glue step.) Center batting pieces, then cardboard, on wrong side of stitched piece. Alternating sides and pulling fabric taut, glue edge of fabric to back of cardboard oval.
6. Beginning and ending at bottom of oval, glue straight edge of lace along edge on wrong side of oval, overlapping ends.
7. Beginning and ending at bottom of oval, glue cord along edge of oval, trimming cord to fit exactly.
8. To cover album, open album flat and place on fabric. Cut fabric 2½″ larger than album on all sides. Press edges of fabric ½″ to wrong side.
9. Place fabric wrong side up on a flat surface. Center opened album on fabric. Fold corners of fabric diagonally over corners of album; glue to secure. Trimming fabric to fit around binder hardware if necessary, fold edges of fabric over edges of album; glue to secure.
10. Glue oval to center front of album.

84

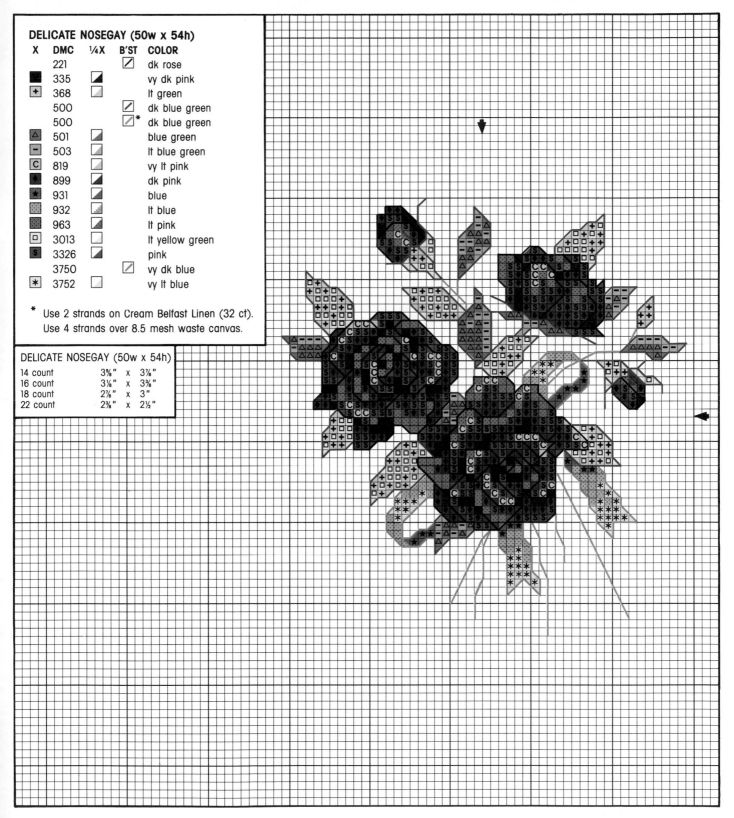

DELICATE NOSEGAY (50w x 54h)

X	DMC	¼X	B'ST	COLOR
	221		☑	dk rose
■	335	◩		vy dk pink
✚	368	◩		lt green
	500		☑	dk blue green
	500		☑*	dk blue green
△	501	◩		blue green
▬	503	◩		lt blue green
C	819	◩		vy lt pink
✹	899	◩		dk pink
★	931	◩		blue
▦	932	◩		lt blue
▨	963	◩		lt pink
▢	3013	▫		lt yellow green
S	3326	◩		pink
	3750		☑	vy dk blue
✳	3752	▫		vy lt blue

* Use 2 strands on Cream Belfast Linen (32 ct).
  Use 4 strands over 8.5 mesh waste canvas.

DELICATE NOSEGAY (50w x 54h)

14 count	3⅝"	x	3⅞"
16 count	3⅛"	x	3⅜"
18 count	2⅞"	x	3"
22 count	2⅜"	x	2½"

Chart, page 94

Image of the Past

Reflecting turn-of-the-century elegance, Paula's view of a lady's bedroom opens a window to the past. We can easily envision a woman of olden times relaxing in such a feminine haven, surrounded by her favorite things. During this private time, she might model a new dress before the mirror or stitch a needlework sampler to adorn the wall. Today, as then, the bedroom is a quiet place to retreat from the world — a place that is uniquely our own. And when this room is appointed with delicate accessories, we find a special pleasure in spending time there. With the ideas shown in this collection, you can create your own gentle refuge with the beauty of the past.

Ribbon and Roses Table, page 100

88

ibbons and roses add an air of romance to the bedroom. Adorned with a pretty painted design, a little table is transformed into a graceful accessory. Ruffled pillows are stacked and tied with a crisp ribbon to create a delightful decorative accent.

Stack of Pretty Pillows, page 105

Delicate touches make the bedroom a cozy haven. Tied with satin ribbon and embellished with a tiny nosegay, little sachet pillows fill the room with fragrance. Bed linens trimmed with lacy crocheted edging invite sweet dreams.

For curling up on cool evenings, a lightweight afghan and matching pillow are appliquéd with hearts cut from vintage floral handkerchiefs.

Sachet Pillows, page 105
Crochet-Trimmed Sheet Set, page 104

Heart Afghan and Heart Pillow, page 99

Embellished Towel Set, page 105
Sachet Bags, page 98
Decorated Soaps, page 104

$\mathscr{F}$or the bath, towels adorned with feminine frills and decorative soaps dressed up with floral motifs will delight the eyes. Dainty sachet bags can be tucked into drawers or the linen closet to keep sheets and towels fragrant.

Soft shadow-quilted flowers grace the yoke of a simple nightgown and a matching lingerie bag. A pretty hanging sachet sweetly scents garments in your closet.

Lingerie Bag, page 103
Shadow-Quilted Gown, page 102
Hanging Sachet, page 98

X	DMC	¼X	½X	B'ST	COLOR	X	DMC	¼X	½X	B'ST	COLOR	X	DMC	¼X	½X	B'ST	COLOR
	blanc			✦ *	white		435				vy dk tan		776			✦	vy lt rose
	ecru				ecru		437				tan		783				dk gold
	221			✦ †	burgundy		501			✦ †	dk blue green		801				dk brown
	309				dk rose		502				blue green		813				sky blue
	312		✦	✦ +	dk blue		503				lt blue green		823				navy
	320				green		504		✦		vy lt blue green		827				lt sky blue
	322		✦	✦ ★	blue		543		✦		vy lt beige brown		831				olive
	326			✦ °	vy dk rose		646			✦	dk grey		839				vy dk beige brown
	334		✦		lt blue		647			✦	grey		840				dk beige brown
	335			✦ °	rose		648				lt grey		841		★		beige brown
	336				vy dk blue		676				lt gold		842				lt beige brown
	340				violet		726				yellow		890			✦ *	vy dk green
	413				charcoal		729				gold		899			✦ ★	lt rose
	433			✦ ★	brown		738				lt tan		928		✦		lt blue grey
	434		✦	✦ ★	lt brown		739				vy lt tan		931			✦ ★	grey blue

X	DMC	¼X	½X	B'ST	COLOR
▣	932				lt grey blue
	938		◢	✱	vy dk brown
▒	963	◢			pink
	3023		◉		beige grey
△	3024	◢	◈	✱	lt beige grey
◆	3350	◢			dk mauve
◉	3731	◢			mauve
▨	3733				lt mauve
✶	3746				dk violet
◇	3755		▲		vy lt blue
■	3799				dk charcoal
●	646	French Knot			dk grey
○	776	French Knot			vy lt rose
◉	3731	French Knot			mauve

◼ Pink area indicates last row of previous section of design.

Note: Mirror reflection and wallpaper stitched with **1** strand of floss.

* White for lace on dress. Vy dk green for hatboxes and leaves on hats. Vy dk brown for all other.
† Burgundy for rug and ribbon on hat. Dk blue green for all other.
+ Use 2 strands of floss.
★ Blue for dress reflection. Brown for floor planks. Lt brown for dress form reflection. Lt rose for flowers in reflection, flowers in window, and sampler. Grey blue for inside of trunk lid and ribbon on sampler. Lt beige grey for all other.
○ Rose for flowers in quilt. Vy dk rose for all other.

IMAGE OF THE PAST (180w x 141h)			
14 count	12⅞"	x	10⅛"
16 count	11¼"	x	8⅞"
18 count	10"	x	7⅞"
22 count	8¼"	x	6½"

Image of the Past (180w x 141h) was stitched over 2 fabric threads on a 23" x 21" piece of Cream Belfast Linen (32 ct). Two strands of floss were used for Cross Stitch, 2 for French Knots, and 1 for all other stitches unless otherwise noted. The design was custom framed.

Continued on pages 96 and 97

HANGING SACHET (Shown on page 93)

You will need two 5″ x 11½″ pieces of fabric for sachet and one 2″ x 7″ piece of fabric for hanging loop, thread to match fabric, two 5″ x 11½″ pieces of white cotton fabric for lining, ½ yd of ⅞″w satin ribbon, embroidery floss for tassel, 2½″ square of cardboard, polyester fiberfill, potpourri, and a small spray of silk flowers.

1. Place sachet fabric pieces right sides together. Place 1 lining fabric piece on wrong side of each sachet fabric piece. Referring to Fig. 1, cut a point at 1 end (bottom) of fabric pieces.

Fig. 1

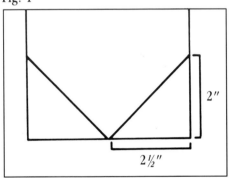

2. Using a ¼″ seam allowance and leaving top edge open, sew pieces together. Cut corners diagonally.
3. Press top edge of bag ¼″ to wrong side; press 2½″ to wrong side again and stitch in place. Turn right side out and press.
4. For hanging loop, match right sides and fold remaining fabric piece in half lengthwise. Using a ¼″ seam allowance, sew long edges together. Turn right side out and press. Matching ends, fold in half to form a loop.

5. Place ends of hanging loop into top of sachet with approx. 2″ of loop extending above sachet; whipstitch ends of loop to inside back of sachet.
6. For tassel, wind floss approx. 30 times around cardboard square. For top of tassel, thread an 8″ length of floss under all strands at 1 end of square; knot tightly and trim ends (Fig. 2). Cut floss at opposite end of square (Fig. 2).

Fig. 2

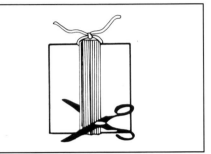

7. To wrap tassel, begin ¼″ from top and tightly wrap an 18″ length of floss around tassel; knot and trim ends.
8. Trim ends of tassel even. Whipstitch top of tassel to bottom point of sachet.
9. Stuff bottom half of sachet with fiberfill; fill with potpourri to 2″ from top.
10. Tie ribbon into a bow around top of sachet; trim ends. Tuck stem of flower spray behind bow.

SACHET BAGS

(Shown on page 92)

For each bag, you will need two 5½″ x 10½″ pieces of fabric for bag, thread to match fabric, two 5½″ x 10½″ pieces of white cotton fabric for lining, desired trim(s) and ribbon(s), fabric glue or thread to match trim(s), and potpourri.

1. Referring to photo, arrange trim(s) as desired on 1 bag fabric piece; trim ends of trim(s) even with edges of fabric. Glue or stitch in place.
2. Place bag fabric pieces right sides together. Place 1 lining fabric piece on wrong side of each bag fabric piece. Using a ¼″ seam allowance, sew pieces together along long edges and 1 short edge (bottom). Cut corners diagonally.
3. Press top edge of bag ¼″ to wrong side; press ¼″ to wrong side again and stitch in place. Turn right side out and press. Fold top edge of bag desired amount to inside.
4. Fill bag with desired amount of potpourri. Tie ribbon(s) into a bow around top of bag.

HEART AFGHAN   (Shown on page 91)

You will need one 45" x 58" piece of Soft White Anne Cloth (18 ct) for afghan, two 2" x 44" strips of fabric (pieced as necessary) for binding, thread to match afghan and binding fabric, two 43" lengths of 4½"w Battenberg lace trim, printed or embroidered handkerchiefs (we found ours at antique shops), embroidery floss, buttons, 1/16"w and 1/8"w satin ribbon, lightweight fusible interfacing, paper-backed fusible web, and tracing paper.

1. Trim selvages from afghan. Press long edges ½" to wrong side; press ½" to wrong side again and stitch in place.
2. Press ends of each binding strip ½" to wrong side. With wrong sides together, press each strip in half lengthwise.
3. (*Note:* Follow Steps 3 and 4 for each raw edge of afghan.) Place afghan wrong side up. Matching straight edge of 1 lace trim length to 1 raw edge of afghan, place lace right side up on afghan. Matching raw edge of binding to straight edge of lace, place 1 binding strip on lace. Using a ¼" seam allowance, sew all layers together along raw edge of binding.
4. Referring to photo, press seam allowance to right side of afghan so that lace extends beyond edge of afghan; press binding to right side of afghan along seamline, covering seam allowance. Stitching along top edge of binding, topstitch binding in place.
5. Trace heart pattern onto tracing paper; cut out.
6. (*Note:* Refer to photo for remaining steps.) For heart appliqués, follow manufacturers' instructions to fuse interfacing, then web, to wrong side of

1 handkerchief. Center pattern over desired motif on handkerchief; pin in place. Cut out heart. Repeat to cut desired number of hearts. Arrange hearts on afghan as desired; fuse in place. Use 3 strands of floss to work Blanket Stitch, page 125, along edge of each heart.
7. Thread ends of an 18" length of desired width ribbon through each button from back to front; tie ends into a bow. Arrange buttons on afghan and stitch in place.

HEART PILLOW
(Shown on page 91)

You will need 1 Soft White Anne Cloth (18 ct) pillow square (approx. 11" square), one 11" square of fabric for backing, one 6" x 90" strip of fabric (pieced as necessary) for ruffle, one 1½" x 45" bias strip of fabric (pieced as necessary) and 1¼ yds of 1/8" dia. cord for cording, thread to match fabrics, 1 printed or embroidered handkerchief (we found ours at an antique shop), embroidery floss, four 5/8" dia. 4-hole buttons, 1⅓ yds of 1/16"w satin ribbon, tapestry needle, ½ yd of 5/8"w satin ribbon for bow, polyester fiberfill, lightweight fusible interfacing, paper-backed fusible web, and tracing paper.

1. To apply heart appliqué to center of Anne Cloth pillow square, follow Steps 5 and 6 of Heart Afghan instructions, this page.
2. For ribbon border, cut 1/16"w ribbon into four equal lengths.
3. (*Note:* Refer to photo for Step 3.) Thread tapestry needle with 1 ribbon length. Beginning at 1 edge of pillow square, work Running Stitch, page 125,

over and under 4 fabric threads along center of 1 "woven stripe." At each "woven stripe" intersection, run ribbon diagonally through 2 holes of 1 button to attach button. Continue to work Running Stitch to opposite edge of pillow square. Repeat for remaining ribbon lengths and buttons. Trim ribbons even with edges of pillow square.
4. For cording, lay cord along center on wrong side of bias strip. Matching long edges, fold strip over cord. Use a zipper foot and machine baste along length of strip close to cord.
5. Matching raw edges and starting 1" from end of cording, baste cording to right side of pillow square, clipping seam allowance as needed. Open 1 end of cording and cut cord to fit exactly. Insert unopened end of cording in opened end; fold raw edge of top fabric ½" to wrong side and baste in place.
6. For ruffle, match right sides and short edges of fabric strip and use a ½" seam allowance to sew short edges together. Press seam open. With wrong sides together, match raw edges and press ruffle in half. Baste 3/8" and ¼" from raw edge. Pull basting threads, drawing up gathers to fit pillow square.
7. Matching raw edges, baste ruffle to right side of pillow square over cording.
8. Place backing fabric and pillow square right sides together. Using zipper foot and leaving an opening for turning, sew pillow square to backing, sewing as close as possible to cording. Cut corners diagonally, turn right side out, and press. Stuff pillow with fiberfill; sew final closure by hand. Remove all visible basting threads.
9. Referring to photo, tie 5/8"w ribbon into a bow around 1 button; trim ends.

RIBBON AND ROSES TABLE (Shown on page 88)

You will need a small unfinished wooden table with top that measures at least 8″ x 10″ (we found our table at a second-hand furniture store and removed the old finish); white semi-gloss alkyd enamel paint; the following colors of artists' oil paints: Titanium White, Cadmium Yellow, Permanent Red, Prussian Blue, Sap Green, and Van Dyke Brown; Oil Colour Liquin by Winsor & Newton; turpentine; foam brushes; #8 and #10 flat paintbrushes; #0 liner paintbrush; plastic palette; palette knife; paper towels; tracing paper; ruler; cheesecloth; fine sandpaper; and tack cloth.

Note: If desired, practice painting on a piece of scrap wood before painting table.

1. Sand table thoroughly; wipe lightly with tack cloth to remove dust.
2. Allowing to dry between coats, use foam brush to paint table with white enamel paint. If necessary, sand and wipe lightly with tack cloth between coats.
3. Follow Tracing Patterns, page 124, to trace heavy lines of bow, rose, and leaf patterns, page 101, onto tracing paper; cut out.
4. Referring to photo, use ruler and a pencil to lightly draw 2 lines 1⅛″ apart for horizontal ribbon on tabletop and sides. Repeat to draw vertical ribbon. Arrange patterns on tabletop; lightly draw around patterns desired number of times. Referring to patterns, lightly draw detail lines where indicated by heavy lines on roses and bow.

5. Use palette knife to mix oil paints on palette as follows:
   Pink mix — Titanium White + Permanent Red
   Lt pink mix — Pink mix + Titanium White
   Blue mix — Prussian Blue + Van Dyke Brown + Titanium White + a dot of Permanent Red
   Lt blue mix — Titanium White + a small amount of blue mix
   Dk blue mix — Blue mix + Prussian Blue
   Lt green mix — Sap Green + Cadmium Yellow
6. (*Note:* Read Painting Techniques before painting table.) Referring to photo and patterns, paint design as follows:
a. Basecoat roses with lt pink mix. Shade with pink mix. For highlights, lift off color with clean brush.
b. Basecoat leaves with lt green mix. Shade with Sap Green.
c. Basecoat ribbons and bow with blue mix, using #8 brush to carefully paint around roses and leaves. Highlight with lt blue mix. Shade with dk blue mix.
d. To freehand small flowers, use corner of #10 brush to paint Titanium White circles for petals. For each flower center, use liner brush to paint a Cadmium Yellow dot, then a smaller Sap Green dot at center of yellow dot.
e. For stems on small flowers, use wooden end of paintbrush to scrape through blue paint, allowing white paint to show through.

7. For pink detail on sides of tabletop and table, add a generous amount of Liquin to remaining pink mix. Being careful to avoid painted ribbon, use cheesecloth to apply paint to sides of tabletop and table; wipe off with clean cheesecloth, leaving pink paint in crevices of woodwork. Repeat with remaining dk blue mix for table legs. Allow to dry.

PAINTING TECHNIQUES
Basecoat: Dip clean #10 brush into Liquin; work well into brush. Load small amount of base color paint on brush; work into brush. Paint, covering lines.

Shading: Do not clean brush after painting basecoat. Corner load darker paint color onto brush; work into brush. Shade where indicated by crosshatching on pattern.

Highlighting (by lifting off color): To lift off color, clean brush thoroughly in turpentine; dry thoroughly with paper towel. Lightly push tips of paintbrush bristles into paint, lifting off color to show white paint underneath. Highlight where indicated by dots on pattern.

Highlighting (by adding color): Do not clean brush after painting basecoat. Corner load lighter paint color onto brush; work into brush. Highlight where indicated by dots on pattern.

ROSES

LEAF

BOW

SHADOW-QUILTED GOWN (Shown on page 93)

Note: For this project, the yoke of a purchased sleeveless nightgown will be removed and replaced with a new yoke and shoulder ties.

You will need a sleeveless white cotton nightgown with front yoke; white sheer cotton organdy and white cotton broadcloth (see Steps 1 and 13 for amounts); one 6″ square each of the following colors of cotton broadcloth: pink, dk pink, rose, purple, lt green, and green; ⅜″w lace trim for top of yoke; 1½″w lace trim for bottom of yoke; a 1¼″w bias strip of fabric and ⅛″ dia. cord for cording; 3 yds of 1½″w white satin ribbon for shoulder ties; white thread; yellow, rose, dk rose, purple, and green embroidery floss; paper-backed fusible web; dressmaker's tracing paper; ballpoint pen; and artists' tracing paper.

1. For shadow-quilted yoke, measure bottom edge of front yoke on gown; add ½″. Cut one 3¾″w piece of organdy and two 3¾″w pieces of white broadcloth the determined measurement.
2. Follow manufacturer's instructions to fuse web to wrong sides of colored broadcloth squares.
3. Trace pattern, page 103, onto artists' tracing paper.
4. For design pieces, refer to pattern and color key, page 103, and use dressmaker's tracing paper and ballpoint pen to transfer parts of design separately onto right sides of colored broadcloth squares. Cut out pieces.
5. Referring to pattern for placement, arrange design pieces at center of 1 white broadcloth piece; fuse in place.
6. To shadow-quilt, place organdy piece over fused fabric; use white

thread and baste securely in place. Referring to photo and working from center of design outward, use a very small Running Stitch, page 125, and 1 strand of coordinating floss to stitch very close to edges of each design piece. Use 3 strands of yellow floss to work 3 French Knots, page 125, at center of each purple flower.
7. With right sides facing and matching straight edge of lace to raw edge of yoke piece, baste ⅜″w lace along side and top edges of quilted yoke piece.
8. Place remaining broadcloth piece and quilted yoke piece right sides together. Using a ¼″ seam allowance, sew all layers together along side and top edges. Cut corners diagonally, turn right side out, and press. Remove any visible basting threads.
9. For cording and bottom lace trim, measure bottom edge of quilted yoke. Cut cord the determined length. Cut bias strip and 1½″w lace 1″ longer than cord. Press ends of bias strip and lace ½″ to wrong side.
10. For cording, lay cord along center on wrong side of bias strip. Matching long edges, fold strip over cord. Use a zipper foot and machine baste along length of strip close to cord. Whipstitch opening closed at each end of cording.
11. Matching right sides and raw edges, baste cording, then lace, along bottom edge of quilted yoke.
12. To attach quilted yoke to gown, pin yoke to gown with right sides facing, matching raw edge of quilted yoke to bottom yoke seamline on gown (Fig. 1). Using zipper foot, sew quilted yoke to gown as close as possible to cording, easing as necessary. Leaving a ¼″ seam allowance, trim original front yoke away from gown. To finish

raw edges, use a medium width zigzag stitch with a short stitch length to stitch over edge of seam allowance. Press quilted yoke to right side; press seam allowance toward bottom of gown.

Fig. 1

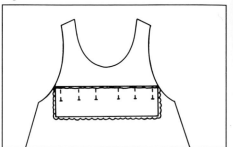

13. For back yoke, measure bottom edge of back yoke of gown; add ½″. (If your gown does not have a back yoke, use a fabric marking pen to draw a line across back of gown even with bottom edge of front yoke. Measure this line and add ½″.) Cut two 3¾″w pieces of white broadcloth the determined measurement.
14. Place yoke pieces right sides together. Using a ¼″ seam allowance, sew pieces together along short edges (sides) and 1 long edge (top). Cut corners diagonally, turn right side out, and press. Baste ¼″ from remaining raw edge (bottom) of yoke.
15. To attach back yoke to gown, repeat Step 12, using a ¼″ seam allowance.
16. Cut ribbon into four 27″ lengths. Press 1 end of each length 1″ to right side. Referring to photo and matching right side of ribbon to wrong side of yoke, sew pressed end of 1 ribbon length inside each top corner of front and back yokes.
17. Tie ribbons into bows to form shoulder straps.

LINGERIE BAG (Shown on page 93)

You will need two 13″ x 18″ pieces of white eyelet fabric; one 4″ x 13″ piece of white sheer cotton organdy; two 4″ x 13″ pieces and two 13″ x 18″ pieces of white cotton broadcloth; one 6″ square each of the following colors of cotton broadcloth: pink, dk pink, rose, purple, lt green, and green; two 13″ lengths of 1½″w lace; two 1¼″ x 13″ bias strips of fabric and two 13″ lengths of ⅛″ dia. cord for cording; 1 yd each of ⅜″w and ½″w white ribbon; yellow, rose, dk rose, purple, and green embroidery floss; white thread; paper-backed fusible web; dressmaker's tracing paper; ballpoint pen; and artists' tracing paper.

1. For shadow-quilted panel, use one 4″ x 13″ broadcloth piece and organdy piece and follow Steps 2 - 6 of Shadow-Quilted Gown instructions, page 102.
2. For each cording length, lay 1 length of cord along center on wrong side of 1 bias strip. Matching long edges, fold strip over cord. Use a zipper foot and machine baste along length of strip close to cord.
3. Matching right sides and raw edges, baste 1 cording length, then 1 lace length, along each long edge of quilted panel.
4. Place quilted panel and remaining 4″ x 13″ white broadcloth piece right sides together. Use zipper foot and sew

pieces together as close as possible to cording along each long edge. Turn right side out and press.
5. For bag, place quilted panel right side up on right side of 1 eyelet fabric piece with bottom cording 4½″ from 1 short edge (bottom) of eyelet fabric; pin in place. Use zipper foot and stitch panel to eyelet along each long edge of organdy as close as possible to cording.
6. (*Note:* Use a ½″ seam allowance for Steps 6 - 8.) Place eyelet pieces right sides together. Leaving top edge open, sew pieces together along side and bottom edges. Cut corners diagonally, turn right side out, and press.
7. For lining, place 13″ x 18″ broadcloth pieces right sides together. Leaving a 3″ long opening in center of 1 long edge, sew along long edges and 1 short edge. Cut corners diagonally. Do not turn right side out.
8. Matching right sides and raw edges, place bag inside lining. Sew lining and bag together along top raw edge. Turn right side out through opening in side of lining; sew final closure by hand. Insert lining into bag and press.
9. For ribbon ties, place ribbon lengths together. Tack centers of ribbons to right edge of bag at seamline 2″ from top of bag. Tie ribbons together into a bow around top of bag.

COLOR KEY
- pink
- dk pink
- rose
- purple
- lt green
- green

CROCHET-TRIMMED SHEET SET (Shown on page 90)

FINISHED SIZE: approx. 1¾"w

SUPPLIES

"Knit-Cro-Sheen" by J. & P. Coats Art. A64/size 10, Crystal Blue *or* any equivalent bedspread weight cotton crochet thread (size 10)
Steel crochet hook, size 6 (1.80 mm)
Rust-proof pins
Sewing needle
Sewing thread to match crochet thread
Flat bed sheet and two pillowcases

ABBREVIATIONS

ch	chain
dc	double crochet(s)
sc	single crochet(s)
sp(s)	space(s)
st	stitch
YO	yarn over

★ – work instructions following ★ as many *more* times as indicated in addition to the first time.

( ) or [ ] – work enclosed instructions *as many* times as specified by the number immediately following *or* work all enclosed instructions in the stitch or space indicated *or* contains explanatory remarks.

EDGING

Ch 8; join with slip st to first ch to form a ring.
Row 1: Ch 4, [dc, (ch 1, dc) 6 times] in ring.
Note: Work Double Crochet Cluster *(abbreviated dc Cluster)* as follows:
★ YO, insert hook in space indicated and pull up a loop, YO and draw through 2 loops on hook; repeat from ★ 2 times *more*, YO and draw through all 4 loops on hook.

Row 2: Ch 3, turn; work dc Cluster in first ch-1 sp, (ch 3, work dc Cluster in next ch-1 sp) across: 7 dc Clusters.
Row 3: Ch 1, turn; sc in first dc Cluster, (ch 5, sc in next dc Cluster) 6 times.
Row 4: Ch 8, turn; skip first ch-5 sp, work (sc, ch 5, sc) in next ch-5 sp; leave remaining ch-5 sps unworked.
Row 5: Ch 4, turn; work [dc, (ch 1, dc) 6 times] in ch-5 sp, sc in ch-8 sp.
Repeat Rows 2 - 5 for pattern until edging is desired length, ending by working Row 3; do not finish off.

HEADING

Row 1: Ch 6 *(counts as first dc plus ch 3)*, dc in ch-3 sp, ★ ch 3, (dc, ch 3) twice in ch-8 sp, dc in next ch-3 sp; repeat from ★ across.
Row 2: Ch 1, turn; sc in first dc, (ch 3, sc in next dc) across.
Row 3: Ch 1, turn; sc in first sc, (ch 5, sc in next sc) across; finish off.

FINISHING

To wash and block edging, use a mild detergent and warm water and gently squeeze suds through edging; do not wring. Rinse several times in cool, clear water. Roll in a clean terry towel and gently press out excess moisture. Lay on a flat surface and shape to proper size; pin in place using rust-proof pins where needed. Allow to dry completely. Referring to photo, place edging on sheet or pillowcase and baste in place. Hand or machine stitch to secure. Remove basting thread.

DECORATED SOAPS
(Shown on page 92)

For each soap, you will need a bar of soap, motif cut from fabric, craft glue, paraffin, double boiler (or electric frying pan and metal can) for melting paraffin, tongs, waxed paper, and newspaper.

1. Glue motif to soap.
2. (*Caution:* Do not melt paraffin over an open flame or directly on burner.) Cover work area with newspaper. Place a layer of waxed paper over newspaper. Melt paraffin over hot water in double boiler or in a can placed in an electric frying pan filled with water.
3. (*Note:* Covering only front of soap with paraffin allows soap to be used without affecting motif.) With motif side down, use tongs to hold soap. Dip soap in paraffin, covering front of soap. Place soap, motif side up, on waxed paper; allow paraffin to harden.
4. Repeat Step 3 to apply a second layer of paraffin to soap.

EMBELLISHED TOWEL SET   (Shown on page 92)

You will need 1 washcloth; 1 hand towel; 1 bath towel; desired fabrics, lace trims, and ribbons; and thread to match fabrics, trims, and ribbons.

Note: Refer to photo for all steps.

WASHCLOTH

1. For fabric trim, cut a 2¾" x 9" strip of fabric. Press long edges ¼" to wrong side.
2. Arrange fabric strip, laces, and ribbons as desired across 1 corner of washcloth; pin in place. Trim ends of trims even with edges of washcloth. Stitch trims in place.
3. To secure raw edges of trims at edges of washcloth, use a medium width zigzag stitch with a medium stitch length to stitch over raw edges of trims.

HAND TOWEL

1. To bind bottom edge of towel, cut a 4"w fabric strip 1" longer than bottom edge of towel. Press ends of strip ½" to wrong side.
2. With right side of fabric facing wrong side of towel, match 1 long edge of strip to bottom edge of towel. Using a 1" seam allowance, sew fabric to towel along bottom edge of towel. Fold fabric over bottom edge of towel to right side of towel; press. Baste raw edge in place.
3. For fabric trim, cut a 3¾"w strip of fabric 1" longer than bottom edge of towel. Press edges ½" to wrong side.
4. Cut laces and ribbons 1" longer than bottom edge of towel. Press ends ½" to wrong side.
5. Referring to photo, arrange fabric strip, laces, and ribbons along bottom of towel, being sure to cover raw edge of binding fabric. Stitch in place.

BATH TOWEL

1. For ruffle, cut a 7½"w fabric strip 2½ times as long as bottom edge of towel. Press ends of strip ½" to wrong side. With wrong sides together, press strip in half lengthwise. Stitch close to each end of strip. Baste ⅜" and ¼" from raw edge. Pull basting threads, drawing up gathers to fit bottom edge of towel.
2. Place ruffle on right side of towel with top edge of ruffle overlapping bottom edge of towel ½"; baste in place.
3. For remaining trims, follow Steps 3 - 5 of Hand Towel instructions, being sure to cover raw edge of ruffle.

STACK OF PRETTY PILLOWS   (Shown on page 89)

You will need two 12½" squares each of 3 different fabrics, 4½ yds of 1"w pregathered lace, thread to match fabrics, polyester fiberfill, and 1½ yds of 1½"w wired ribbon.

1. Cut lace into three 1½ yd lengths. Press ends ¼" to wrong side.
2. (*Note:* Follow Steps 2 and 3 for each pillow.) Matching straight edge of lace to raw edge of fabric, baste 1 length of lace to right side of 1 fabric square.
3. Place matching fabric squares right sides together. Using a ¼" seam allowance and leaving an opening for turning, sew squares together. Cut corners diagonally, turn right side out, and press. Stuff pillow with fiberfill. Sew final closure by hand.
4. Referring to photo, stack pillows together; wrap ribbon around pillows and tie into a bow.

SACHET PILLOWS   (Shown on page 90)

For each set of 3 pillows, you will need three 5½" x 10½" pieces from different fabrics for pillows, thread to match fabrics, three 5½" x 10½" pieces of white cotton fabric for pillow linings, 1½ yds of ½"w satin ribbon, polyester fiberfill, potpourri, and a small spray of silk flowers.

1. (*Note:* Follow Steps 1 and 2 to make each pillow.) Place 1 pillow fabric piece and 1 lining fabric piece wrong sides together. With lining side out, match short edges and fold fabric pieces in half. Using a ¼" seam allowance and leaving an opening for turning, sew pieces together along raw edges. Cut corners diagonally, turn right side out, and press.
2. Sprinkle desired amount of potpourri into pillow. Stuff pillow with fiberfill. Sew final closure by hand.
3. Referring to photo, stack pillows together; wrap ribbon around pillows and tie into a bow. Tuck stem of flower spray under bow.

Summer Comes Calling

In this nostalgic piece, Paula recaptures a time when the front porch was a favorite gathering spot on summer evenings. After supper, the entire family could often be found there enjoying the cool breeze and visiting with neighbors, sometimes lingering long past dusk. A rocking chair plumped with pillows was a comfortable place for Mama to relax and catch up on her mending. The old porch swing, draped with a homey quilt, was the site of many summer courtships (conducted under Papa's watchful eye, of course). For many of us today, gentle evening breezes inspire memories of the pleasures to be had when summer comes calling.

Chart, page 114

Porch Swing, page 121

*W*ith *their bright yellow petals, sunflowers have always been summertime favorites. The bold blossoms add a touch of whimsy to a porch swing (you can use the same painting technique to dress up other wooden lawn furniture, too). Patchwork hearts and summer flowers displayed on a rustic vine wreath reflect two of Grandma's proud accomplishments — expert quilting and beautiful flower gardens.*

Quilted Heart Wreath, page 119

oday, as in years past, country porches often boast pots of showy geraniums. These popular flowers are recreated with paint to add old-fashioned prettiness to a plain T-shirt. More of the blossoms bring a splash of color to a country mailbox.

Geranium Shirt, page 121
Mailbox, page 122

Inspired by one of the quilts in Paula's painting, this coverlet is scattered with delightful pink dogwood blossoms. The flowers are stenciled, then accented with embroidery stitches for an appliquéd look that's quick to create. You'll probably want to sit out on your own front porch while working on the embroidery!

Dogwood Coverlet, page 120

Welcome Sign, page 119

Cheery sunflowers bring summer's charm to any season. Adorning a painted welcome sign, they invite friends and neighbors to feel right at home — even in your garden! An arrangement of the sunny blossoms crafted from twisted paper brightens a table or corner, and a painted floorcloth pairs them harmoniously with colorful geraniums.

Paper Sunflowers, page 118
Floorcloth, page 122

X	DMC	¼X	½X	B'ST	COLOR	X	DMC	¼X	½X	B'ST	COLOR	X	DMC	¼X	B'ST	COLOR
	blanc				white		470	¼X			yellow green		712			cream
	ecru				ecru		471	¼X			lt yellow green		725	¼X		yellow
	319			✓*	vy dk green		500				vy dk blue green		726			lt yellow
	320	¼X			green		501		△	✓+	dk blue green		727			vy lt yellow
	347	¼X			vy dk rose		502	¼X			blue green		729	¼X		dk gold
	355				dk rust		503				lt blue green		738	¼X		lt tan
	356	¼X			rust		543				lt beige brown		739	¼X		vy lt tan
	367	¼X			dk green		640			✓*	dk beige grey		746			vy lt gold
	368	¼X			lt green		642			✓+	beige grey		760			rose
	368				lt green		644				lt beige grey		761	¼X		lt rose
	369				vy lt green		645				dk grey		781		✓‡	vy dk yellow
	433	¼X		✓†	brown		646				grey		783			dk yellow
	434				lt brown		647				lt grey		815		✓§	red
	435			✓★	vy dk tan		648				vy lt grey		822			vy lt beige grey
	436				dk tan		676				gold		840	¼X	✓★	vy dk beige brown
	436	¼X			dk tan		677				lt gold		841	¼X	✓†	dk beige brown
	437	¼X	☆		tan		680	¼X			vy dk gold		842	¼X		beige brown

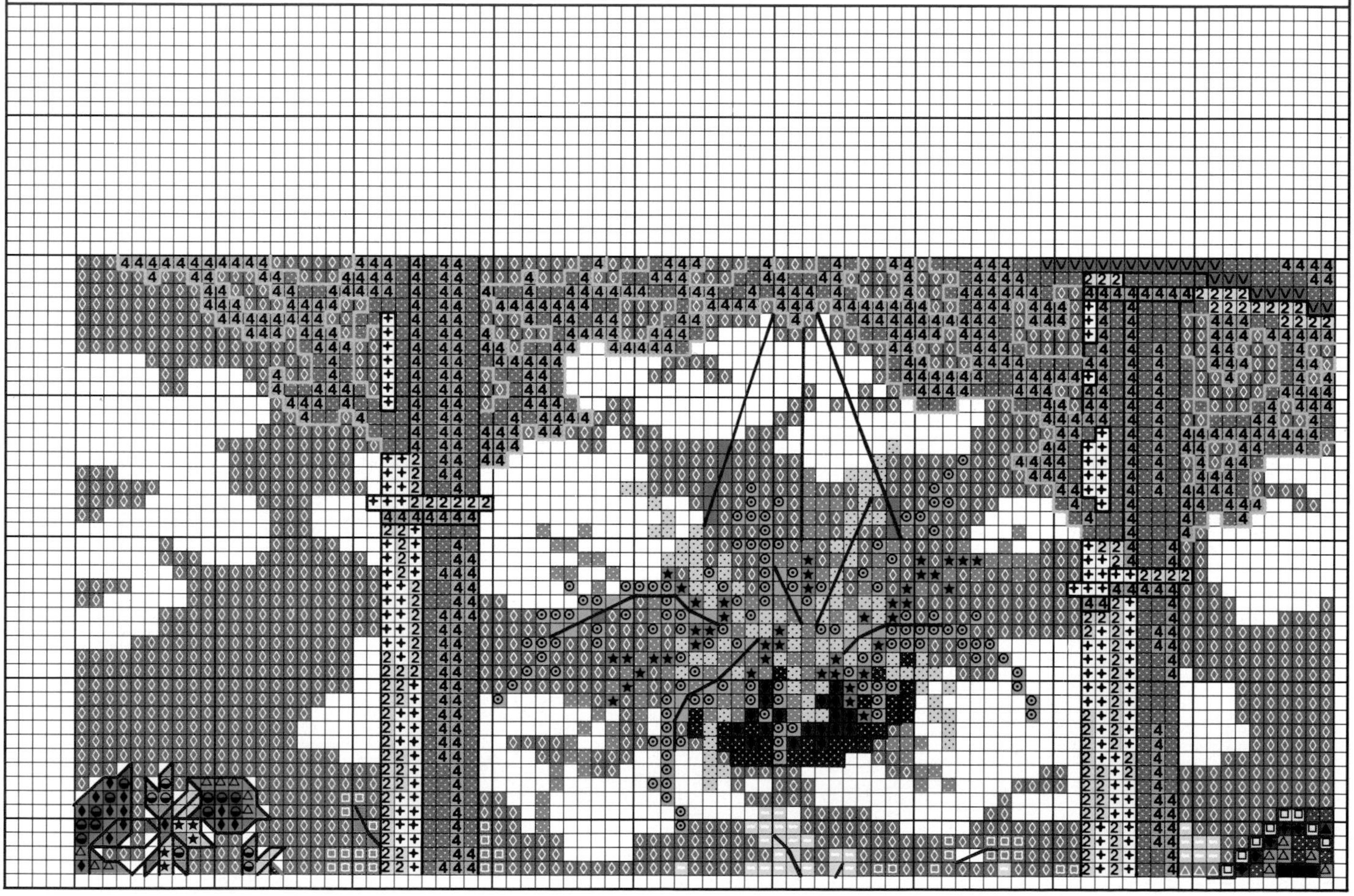

X	DMC	¼X	½X	B'ST	COLOR
◢	844			✎ ‡	vy dk grey
■	898	◢			dk brown
▲	930	◢		✎ °	dk grey blue
◔	931	◢			grey blue
4	932	◢			lt grey blue
	938			✎ §	vy dk brown
✶	3328	◢		✎ ★	dk rose
▨	3346	◢			dk yellow green
★	3362	◢			vy dk yellow green
	3688		▣		mauve
	3750	◢		✎ °	vy dk grey blue
2	3752	☐			vy lt grey blue
	3753		◇		lt blue
▲	3777	◢			vy dk rust
☆	3778				lt rust

Pink area indicates last row of previous section of design.

* Vy dk green for leaves and stems. Dk beige grey for all other.

• Use 1 strand of floss.

† Dk beige brown for quilt. Brown for all other.

★ Vy dk tan for decorative woodwork and walls. Dk rose for appliqué quilt and fabric in basket. Vy dk beige brown for all other.

+ Dk blue green for leaves and stems. Beige grey for quilt in rocking chair. Use 2 strands of beige grey for appliqué quilt.

‡ Vy dk yellow for sunflowers and fabric in basket. Vy dk grey for all other.

§ Vy dk brown for sunflowers, basket, rocking chair, and spool. Red for all other.

° Dk grey blue for quilt. Vy dk grey blue for all other.

SUMMER COMES CALLING (180w x 132h)		
14 count	12⅞"	x 9½"
16 count	11¼"	x 8¼"
18 count	10"	x 7⅜"
22 count	8¼"	x 6"

Summer Comes Calling (180w x 132h) was stitched over 2 fabric threads on a 21" x 18" piece of Cream Belfast Linen (32 ct). Two strands of floss were used for Cross Stitch and 1 for all other stitches unless otherwise noted. The design was custom framed.

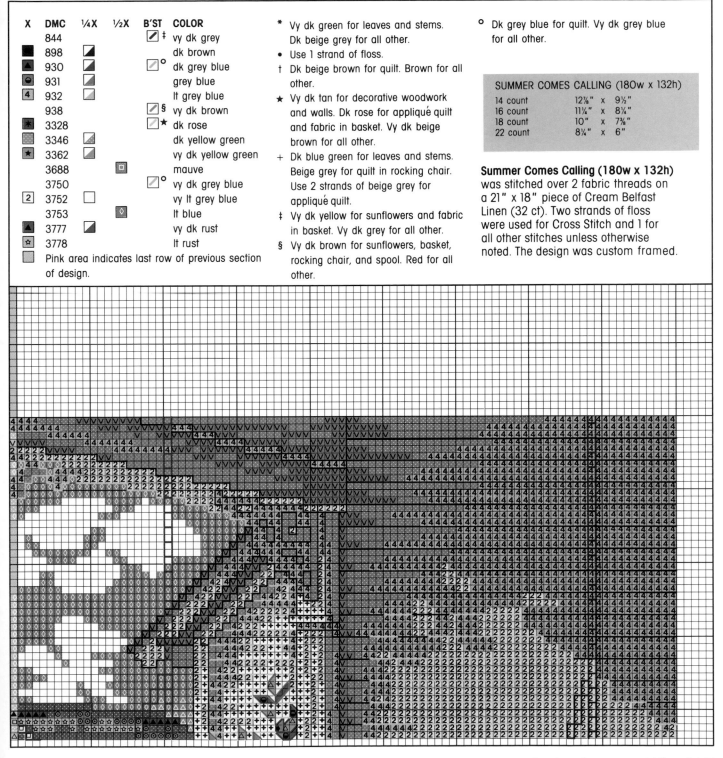

Continued on pages 116 and 117

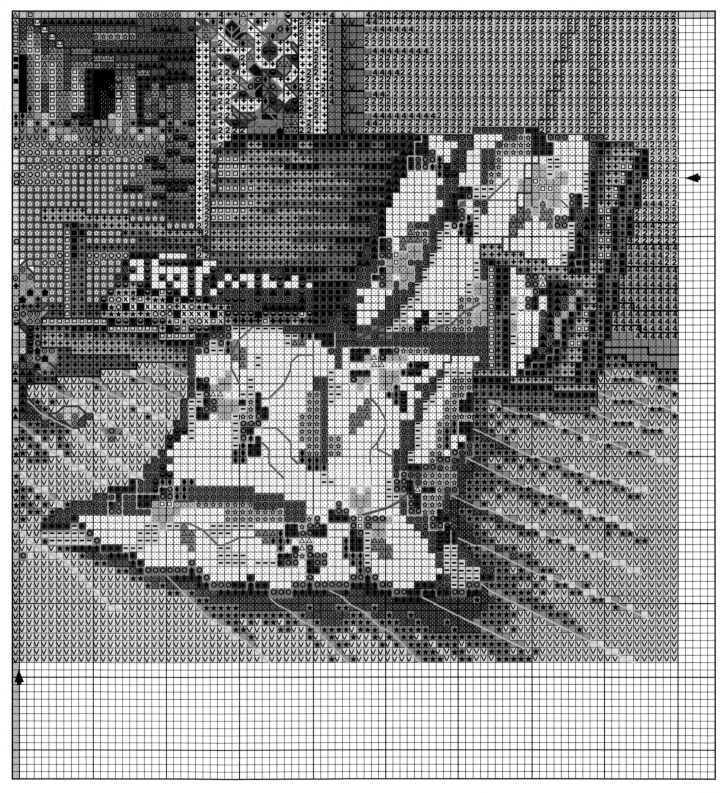

PAPER SUNFLOWERS (Shown on page 113)

For each flower, you will need yellow, brown, and green Paper Capers™ twisted paper (untwisted); 3¾" dia. plastic foam half ball; matte dk yellow spray paint; Design Master® glossy wood tone spray (available at craft stores); 16-gauge florist wire for flower stem; 24-gauge florist wire for leaf stems; wire cutters; green crepe florist tape; compass; tracing paper; craft glue; and artificial ladybug (optional).

1. (*Note:* Refer to photo to assemble flower. Allow to dry after each glue step.) For flower center, cut an 8" length from brown paper. Glue paper over round side of half ball, smoothing wrinkles. Trim excess paper even with flat side (bottom) of half ball.

2. For "fringe" around flower center, cut four 3" lengths from brown paper.

3. For each fringe length, match cut edges and fold one 3" paper length in half. Beginning at cut edges, make cuts ⅛" apart through both layers to within ¼" of fold.

4. Matching fold of paper to bottom edge of half ball, glue 1 fringe length to side of half ball. Overlapping fringe lengths evenly, repeat to glue remaining fringe lengths around half ball.

5. For petal and leaf piece patterns, follow Tracing Patterns, page 124.

6. For petals, cut a 75" length from yellow paper. Lightly spritz both sides of paper with dk yellow paint, then wood tone spray. Allow to dry. Cut paper into fifteen 5" lengths.

7. For each petal section, fold 1 short edge of one 5" paper length 1¾" to 1 side. Using fold as a guide, fanfold paper. Matching dotted lines of pattern to folded edges of paper, place pattern on folded paper. Use a pencil to draw around pattern. Cutting through all layers, cut out petals along solid lines only. Unfold paper and lay flat. Trim off any partial petals.

8. To attach petal sections to flower center, pinch straight edge (bottom) of 1 petal section, gathering edge to approx. 2½". Matching bottom edge of petal section to bottom edge of flower center, glue section to side of flower center. Overlapping sections evenly, repeat to glue remaining petal sections around flower center.

9. For back of flower, cut an 8" length from green paper. Lightly spritz both sides of paper with wood tone spray. Allow to dry.

10. Use compass to draw a 7" dia. circle on paper; cut out. Cut irregular notches approx. ¾" deep into edge of circle. Center and glue circle to back of flower. Smooth excess paper flat against sides of flower; glue in place.

11. For leaves, cut a 24" length from green paper. Lightly spritz both sides of paper with wood tone spray. Allow to dry.

12. Use pattern and cut 4 leaf pieces from green paper. Cut two 8" lengths from 24-gauge wire.

13. For each leaf, place 1 wire length on 1 leaf piece as shown in Fig. 1; glue to secure. With wire between pieces, glue 2 leaf pieces together. Wrap leaf stem with florist tape.

Fig. 1

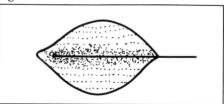

14. For flower stem, cut two 18" lengths from 16-gauge wire. Place lengths side by side and twist together. Insert 1 end of wire lengths 1" into center back of flower; glue to secure. Wrap stem with tape, attaching leaves at desired intervals.

15. Referring to photo, arrange leaves and, if desired, glue ladybug to flower.

LEAF PIECE

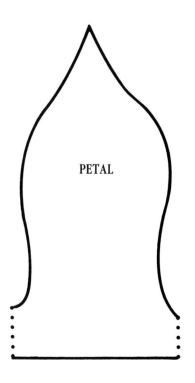

PETAL

QUILTED HEART WREATH

(Shown on page 109)

You will need a 21″ dia. vine wreath, two 9″ squares cut from an old quilt, polyester bonded batting, medium weight cardboard, desired silk or preserved flowers and greenery (we used 4″ dia. silk sunflowers, silk geraniums with leaves, and preserved springerii fern), 2½ yds of desired ribbon, tracing paper, fabric glue, hot glue gun, and glue sticks.

1. For heart pattern, follow Tracing Patterns, page 124.
2. Use pattern and cut 2 hearts each from cardboard and batting.
3. For each quilted heart, use a pencil to draw around 1 cardboard heart on back of 1 quilt square. Cut out heart 1″ outside drawn line. Clip edges of heart to within ¼″ of drawn line. Center 1 batting piece, then cardboard, on back of quilt heart. Alternating sides and pulling fabric taut, use fabric glue to glue clipped edges of heart to back of cardboard. Allow to dry.
4. Referring to photo, arrange greenery, flowers, ribbon, and hearts on wreath; hot glue in place.

HEART

WELCOME SIGN   (Shown on page 112)

You will need an 18½″ length of unfinished 1 x 6 fence board; two 8″ long and two 22″ long twigs; 2″h lettering stencils; black permanent felt-tip pen with fine point; black waterbase stain; off-white, yellow, dk yellow, brown, lt green, and olive green acrylic paint; paintbrushes; tracing paper; graphite transfer paper; cheesecloth; old terry towel; sawtooth hanger; hammer and small nails; and satin-finish polyurethane spray.

1. (*Note:* Refer to photo for all steps.) To "age" board, soak cheesecloth in water and use wet cheesecloth to apply stain to board; wipe off excess with terry towel. Allow to dry.
2. Trace flower patterns onto tracing paper. Use transfer paper to transfer patterns to rough side of board.
3. Using a pencil and stencils, draw outlines of letters on board to spell "WELCOME."
4. Use black pen to draw over transferred lines and pencil lines.
5. To paint letters, mix 1 part off-white paint with 1 part water. Allowing to dry between coats, apply several coats of paint to letters.
6. Paint flowers the following colors, shading or highlighting while basecoat is still wet:
   Flower centers — brown basecoat highlighted with yellow
   Petals — yellow basecoat shaded with dk yellow
   Leaves and stems — lt green basecoat shaded with olive green
Allow to dry.
7. Allowing to dry between coats, apply 2 coats of polyurethane spray to sign.
8. Nail sawtooth hanger to top center back of sign. Nail twigs to edges of sign.

DOGWOOD COVERLET   (Shown on page 111)

For a twin-size coverlet (approx. 69½" x 89"), you will need 4½ yds of 90"w unbleached muslin fabric; ¾ yd of 44"w fabric for binding; a twin size piece (72" x 90") of polyester bonded quilt batting; thirty-two ¾" dia. lt yellow buttons; dk pink, dk green, tan, and yellow embroidery floss; acetate for stencils (available at craft or art supply stores); permanent felt-tip pen with fine point; craft knife; cutting mat or a thick layer of newspapers; removable tape (optional); stencil brushes; paper towels; pink, green, and tan fabric paint; yardstick; compass; safety pins; embroidery hoop; white eraser; and lightweight cardboard.

1. Wash, dry, and press fabrics according to paint manufacturer's recommendations.
2. For coverlet top and backing, cut 2 pieces of muslin same size as batting.
3. Place 1 muslin piece (top) on a flat protected surface. Referring to Diagram A, page 121, use yardstick and a pencil to lightly mark dots and diagonal lines on muslin.
4. Follow Step 1 of Stenciling, page 124, to make flower, stem, small leaf, and large leaf stencils.
5. (*Note:* Follow Step 2 of Stenciling, page 124, for Step 5.) Referring to Diagram B, page 121, and using dots and lines for placement, stencil pink flowers and tan stems on muslin; randomly stencil green leaves on muslin. Erase any visible pencil marks.

6. If necessary, heat-set paint according to manufacturer's recommendations.
7. Matching edges, place batting, then stenciled top (right side up) on remaining muslin piece (backing). Avoiding painted areas, use safety pins spaced 3" to 4" apart to pin all layers together.
8. (*Note:* Refer to photo for colors and placement of stitches. Use 3 strands of floss and stitch through all layers. Refer to Embroidery instructions, page 125, for stitches.) Insert pinned layers in hoop. Work Blanket Stitch along edge of each petal and leaf. Work Stem Stitch along each stem and for detail lines on leaves. Work long straight stitches for detail lines on petals.
9. Use yellow embroidery floss to sew 1 button at center of each flower.
10. For scalloped border template, use compass to draw a 10½" dia. circle on cardboard; cut out. Insert a pin through center of template.
11. (*Note:* Refer to Diagram B, page 121, for Steps 11 - 13.) For scallops next to flowers along edge of coverlet top, insert template pin in each button and use pencil and template to lightly draw a scallop.
12. For each remaining scallop, mark a dot halfway between centers of 2 adjacent flowers. Insert template pin through dot and draw a scallop (scallops should intersect).

13. To complete scallops, refer to Fig. 1 and use template to draw small inward curves where scallops intersect.

Fig. 1

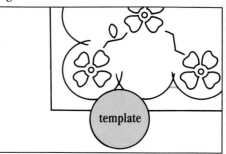

14. Erase any excess lines. Machine baste along scalloped line. Trim coverlet to ¼" from basting line. Remove pins.
15. For binding, cut a 2"w bias strip of fabric 9 yds long (pieced as necessary). Matching wrong sides, press strip in half lengthwise; press each long edge to center.
16. Unfold 1 end of binding; press end ½" to wrong side; refold. Unfold 1 long edge of binding. Beginning with pressed end of binding and matching right side of binding to front of coverlet, pin unfolded edge of binding along edge of coverlet. Continue pinning binding around coverlet until ends of binding overlap ½"; trim excess binding. Using pressed line closest to raw edge as a guide, sew binding to coverlet. Fold binding over raw edges to back of coverlet; whipstitch in place.

DOGWOOD COVERLET
(Continued)

DIAGRAM A

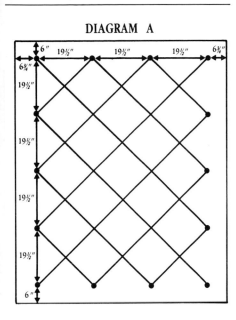

DIAGRAM B

PORCH SWING   (Shown on page 108)

You will need a wooden porch swing with slats close together; flat white latex paint; yellow, dk yellow, pink, dk pink, blue, green, dk green, lt brown, and brown acrylic paint; yardstick; acetate for stencils (available at craft or art supply stores); cutting mat or a thick layer of newspapers; craft knife; removable tape (optional); stencil brushes; paper towels; white eraser; small round paintbrush; two 2″w flat paintbrushes; fine sandpaper; tack cloth; satin-finish polyurethane; compass; and supplies listed in Sponge Painting instructions, page 123.

1. Sand porch swing and wipe lightly with tack cloth to remove dust.
2. Allowing to dry and sanding if necessary between coats, apply 2 coats of latex paint to swing.
3. (*Note:* Refer to photo for Steps 3 - 10.) For borders, use yardstick and a pencil to lightly draw lines ½″ apart for stripes and 1″ squares for checkerboard on swing.
4. Use ½″ strip, square, small sunflower petal, circle, large sunflower leaf, and small sunflower leaf patterns, page 123, and follow Sponge Painting, page 123, to paint borders and sunflowers on swing.
5. Use small round paintbrush to paint stems dk green. Allow to dry.
6. Erase any visible pencil markings.
7. Follow Step 1 of Stenciling, page 124, to make bow and bow gather stencils.
8. With bow knot centered on swing, use pink paint and follow Step 2 of Stenciling, page 124, to stencil half of bow, including knot, onto swing. Use dk pink to shade edges.

9. Reverse bow stencil. With bow knot of stencil positioned over stenciled bow knot on swing, repeat Step 8 to stencil remainder of bow.
10. Using dk pink paint, repeat Steps 8 and 9 to stencil bow gathers over bow.
11. Allowing to dry and sanding if necessary between coats, apply 2 coats of polyurethane to swing.

GERANIUM SHIRT
(Shown on page 110)

You will need a long-sleeved white T-shirt; white, pink, dk pink, green, and dk green fabric paint; 1 yd each of desired ribbons for bow; T-shirt form or cardboard covered with waxed paper; safety pin; removable fabric marking pen; small round paintbrush; and supplies listed in Sponge Painting instructions, page 123.

1. Wash, dry, and press T-shirt according to paint manufacturer's recommendations. Insert T-shirt form into shirt.
2. (*Note:* Refer to photo for Steps 2 - 5.) Use geranium petal, geranium outer leaf, and geranium inner leaf patterns, page 122, and follow Sponge Painting, page 123, to paint geraniums on shirt.
3. Use paintbrush to paint stems green. Allow to dry.
4. Remove any visible pen lines.
5. Tie ribbon lengths together into a bow. Use safety pin on wrong side of shirt to pin bow to shirt.
6. To launder, remove bow and follow paint manufacturer's recommendations.

BOW GATHERS

BOW

FLOORCLOTH (Shown on page 113)

You will need a 35½" x 47½" piece of artist's canvas primed on both sides (available at art supply stores); white, yellow, dk yellow, pink, dk pink, blue, green, dk green, lt brown, and brown acrylic paint; household cement; rolling pin; small round paintbrush; yardstick; white eraser; compass; satin-finish spray varnish; and supplies listed in Sponge Painting instructions, page 123.

1. To finish edges of canvas, measure 3" from each corner along both edges; mark with a pencil. Draw a diagonal line across each corner connecting marks. Cut off corners along drawn lines. Fold top, bottom, and side edges of canvas 1½" to back; secure with cement. Use rolling pin to flatten folded edges. Allow to dry.

2. Refer to Diagram and use yardstick and a pencil to lightly draw lines for borders on canvas.
3. (*Note:* Refer to photo for Steps 3 and 4.) Use geranium petal, geranium outer leaf, and geranium inner leaf patterns, this page, and ¾" strip, square, circle, and large sunflower petal patterns, page 123, and follow Sponge Painting, page 123, to paint borders, sunflowers, and geraniums on floorcloth.
4. Use paintbrush to paint geranium stems dk green. Allow to dry.
5. Erase any visible pencil markings.
6. Allowing to dry between coats, apply 2 coats of varnish to floorcloth.
7. Clean gently with a damp cloth as needed. Store flat or roll with painted side inside.

DIAGRAM

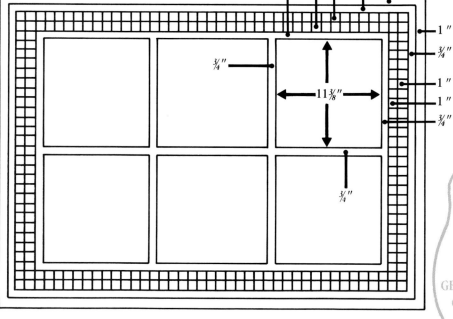

MAILBOX

(Shown on page 110)

You will need a metal mailbox; 2"h script lettering stencils; white spray paint; white, pink, dk pink, green, dk green, and burgundy acrylic paint; foam brush; small round paintbrush; satin-finish polyurethane spray; white eraser; screwdriver (to remove flag and holder); and supplies listed in Sponge Painting instructions, page 123.

1. Remove flag and holder. Use foam brush to paint flag green. Spray paint mailbox white. Allow to dry.
2. (*Note:* Refer to photo for Steps 2 - 4.) Use a pencil and stencils to lightly trace outlines of letters for name onto mailbox. If desired, draw lines connecting letters. Use small round paintbrush to paint letters burgundy. Allow to dry.
3. Use geranium petal, geranium outer leaf, and geranium inner leaf patterns and follow Sponge Painting, page 123, to paint geraniums on mailbox.
4. Use paintbrush to paint stems dk green. Allow to dry.
5. Erase any visible pencil markings.
6. Allowing to dry between coats, apply 2 coats of polyurethane spray to mailbox and flag.
7. Reattach flag and holder to mailbox.

GERANIUM PETAL
(make 3)

GERANIUM
INNER
LEAF

GERANIUM
OUTER
LEAF

SPONGE PAINTING

You will need Miracle Sponges™ (dry, compressed sponges; available at craft stores), tracing paper, permanent felt-tip pen with fine point, plastic or coated paper plates, paper towels, and supplies listed in project instructions.

GENERAL INSTRUCTIONS

1. Trace indicated patterns onto tracing paper and cut out.
2. To make sponge shapes, use pen to draw around patterns on sponges. Use scissors to cut out sponge shapes along drawn lines.
3. To paint with sponge shape, wet sponge to expand; squeeze out excess water. Pour paint on plate. Dip sponge in paint; do not saturate. Dab sponge on paper towels to remove excess paint. Keeping sponge level, place sponge on surface to be painted. Lightly press on sponge with palm of hand. Carefully lift sponge. Allow to dry.

BORDERS

1. For stripes, use indicated strip sponge and green paint to paint between drawn lines, overlapping ends of painted strips slightly.
2. For checkerboard, use 1″ square sponge and blue paint to paint alternating drawn squares.

SUNFLOWERS

1. For each sunflower, determine placement of center of sunflower; use compass to lightly draw a 3″ dia. circle for small sunflower center (porch swing) or a 4¾″ dia. circle for large sunflower center (floorcloth).
2. For petals, dip top half (pointed half) of petal sponge in dk yellow paint and bottom half in yellow paint. Overlapping sides of painted petals slightly and overlapping bottoms of petals ¼″ over edge of drawn circle, paint petals around circle.

3. For center, dip half of circle sponge in lt brown paint and half in brown paint. Overlapping edges of painted circles and overlapping bottoms of petals approx. ¼″, use circle sponge to paint center.
4. For porch swing only, use pencil to lightly draw flower stems on swing. Use large and small sunflower leaf sponges and green and dk green paint to paint leaves where desired.

GERANIUMS

1. For geranium petals, use a separate petal sponge for each color and paint a cluster of dk pink, pink, and white petals, overlapping painted petals.
2. Use pencil or fabric marking pen to lightly draw geranium stems.
3. For each geranium leaf, use outer leaf sponge to paint green outer leaf. Use inner leaf sponge to paint dk green inner leaf over outer leaf.

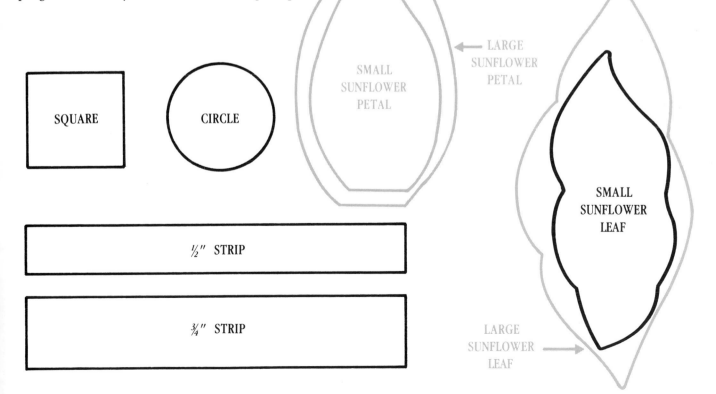

SQUARE

CIRCLE

SMALL SUNFLOWER PETAL

LARGE SUNFLOWER PETAL

SMALL SUNFLOWER LEAF

LARGE SUNFLOWER LEAF

½″ STRIP

¾″ STRIP

GENERAL INSTRUCTIONS

TRACING PATTERNS

When one-half of pattern (indicated by dashed line on pattern) is shown, fold tracing paper in half and place fold along dashed line of pattern. Trace pattern half, marking all placement symbols and markings; turn folded paper over and draw over all markings. Unfold pattern and lay flat. Cut out pattern.

When entire pattern is shown, place tracing paper over pattern and trace pattern, marking all placement symbols and markings. Cut out pattern.

STENCILING

1. For each stencil, cut a piece of acetate 1″ larger on all sides than entire pattern. Center acetate over pattern and use a permanent felt-tip pen with fine point to trace pattern. Place acetate piece on cutting mat and use craft knife to cut out stencil, making sure edges are smooth.
2. Hold or tape stencil in place. Use a clean, dry stencil brush for each color of paint. Dip brush in paint and remove excess paint on a paper towel. Brush should be almost dry to produce good results. Beginning at edge of cutout area, apply paint in a stamping motion. If desired or indicated in instructions, shade design by stamping additional paint or a darker shade of paint around edge of cutout area. Carefully remove stencil and allow paint to dry. To reverse stencil design, clean stencil thoroughly and turn stencil over.

CROSS STITCH

COUNTED CROSS STITCH

Work 1 Cross Stitch to correspond to each colored square on the chart. For horizontal rows, work stitches in 2 journeys (Fig. 1a). For vertical rows, complete each stitch as shown in Fig. 1b. When working over 2 fabric threads, work Cross Stitch as shown in Fig. 1c. When the chart shows a Backstitch crossing a colored square (Fig. 1d), a Cross Stitch (Fig. 1a, 1b, or 1c) should be worked first; then the Backstitch (Fig. 4) should be worked on top of the Cross Stitch.

Fig. 1a

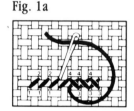

Fig. 1b

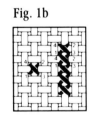

Fig. 1c

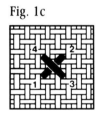

Fig. 1d

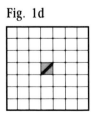

QUARTER STITCH (¼X)

Quarter Stitches are denoted by triangular shapes of color on the chart and on the color key. Come up at 1 (Fig. 2a); then split fabric thread to go down at 2. Fig. 2b shows this technique when working over 2 fabric threads.

Fig. 2a

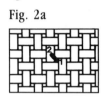

Fig. 2b

HALF CROSS STITCH (½X)

This stitch is 1 journey of the Cross Stitch and is worked from lower left to upper right. Fig. 3 shows the Half Cross Stitch worked over 2 fabric threads.

Fig. 3

BACKSTITCH

For outline detail, Backstitch (shown on chart and color key by black or colored straight lines) should be worked after the design has been completed (Fig. 4).

Fig. 4

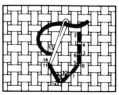

CROSS STITCH (Continued)

WORKING ON LINEN

Using a hoop is optional when working on linen. Roll excess fabric from left to right until stitching area is in proper position. Use the sewing method when working over 2 threads. To use the sewing method, keep your stitching hand on the right side of the fabric; take the needle down and up with 1 stroke. To add support to stitches, place the first Cross Stitch on the fabric with the stitch 1-2 beginning and ending where a vertical fabric thread crosses over a horizontal fabric thread (Fig. 5).

Fig. 5

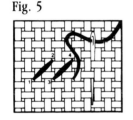

EMBROIDERY

FRENCH KNOT

Bring needle up at 1. Wrap thread once around needle and insert needle at 2, holding end of thread with non-stitching fingers (Fig. 1). Tighten knot; then pull needle through fabric, holding thread until it must be released. For a larger knot, use more strands; wrap only once.

Fig. 1

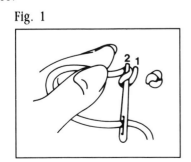

LAZY DAISY STITCH

Following Fig. 2, come up at 1 and make a counterclockwise loop with the thread. Go down at 1 and come up at 2, keeping the thread below the point of the needle. Secure loop by bringing thread over loop and going down at 2.

Fig. 2

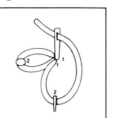

BLANKET STITCH

Referring to Fig. 3a, come up at 1. Go down at 2 and come up at 3, keeping the thread below the point of the needle. Continue working in this manner, going down at even numbers and coming up at odd numbers (Fig. 3b).

Fig. 3a

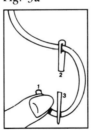

Fig. 3b

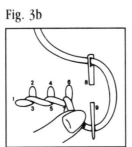

STEM STITCH

Following Fig. 4, come up at 1. Keeping the thread below the stitching line, go down at 2 and come up at 3. Go down at 4 and come up at 5.

Fig. 4

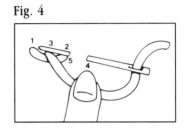

RUNNING STITCH

Make a series of straight stitches with stitch length equal to the space between stitches (Fig. 5).

Fig. 5

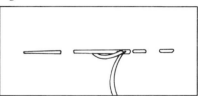

Continued on page 126

GENERAL INSTRUCTIONS (Continued)

QUILTING

Thread quilting needle with an 18″ length of quilting thread; knot 1 end. Bring needle up through all layers of fabric and batting; when knot catches on back of quilt, give thread a short quick pull to pop knot through backing fabric into batting (Fig. 1a). To quilt, use small Running Stitches that are equal in length (Fig. 1b). At the end of a length of thread, knot thread close to top fabric and take needle down through all layers of fabric and batting; when knot catches on top of quilt, pop knot through top fabric into batting. Clip thread close to fabric.

Fig. 1a

Fig. 1b

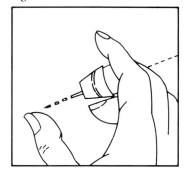

CROCHET

SINGLE CROCHET

To begin a single crochet, insert hook into ridge of chain or under V of stitch. Hook yarn and draw through (Fig. 1a). There are now 2 loops on hook (Fig. 1b). Hook yarn and draw through the 2 loops on hook. One single crochet is now complete.

Fig. 1a

Fig. 1b

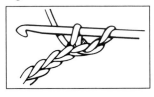

DOUBLE CROCHET

To begin a double crochet, wind yarn once over hook, bringing yarn from back over top of hook. Insert hook into ridge of chain or under V of stitch. Hook yarn and draw through. There are now 3 loops on hook (Fig. 2a). Hook yarn again and draw through the first 2 loops on hook (Fig. 2b); 2 loops remain on hook. Hook yarn again and draw through remaining 2 loops (Fig. 2c). One double crochet is now complete.

Fig. 2a

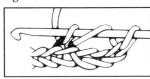

Fig. 2b

Fig. 2c

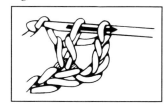

CREDITS

We want to extend a warm thank you to the generous people who allowed us to photograph our projects at their homes:

- *Stolen Moment* and *Summer Comes Calling*: John and Anne Childs
- *Gentle Pastime*: Dr. Reed and Becky Thompson
- *Delicate Beauties:* Dr. Dan and Sandra Cook
- *Image of the Past*: The Clawson Residence

To Magna IV Engravers of Little Rock, Arkansas, we say thank you for the superb color reproduction and excellent pre-press preparation.

We especially want to thank photographers Ken West of Peerless Photography and Jerry R. Davis of Jerry Davis Photography, all of Little Rock, Arkansas, for their time, patience, and excellent work.

To Nelda and Carlton Newby of Creative Framers of North Little Rock, Arkansas, we extend our appreciation for their skillful custom framing.

A special word of thanks goes to Jane Chandler for her beautiful needlework adaptations of Paula's paintings and for creating the *Delicate Nosegay* design on page 85.

We would also like to thank Donna Brown Hill and Pam Fuller Young for their invaluable help with our cross stitch charts.

We extend a sincere thank you to all the people who assisted in making and testing the projects in this book: Jennie Black, Frances Blackburn, Carrie Clifford, Nora Faye Spencer Clift, Wanda Fite, Bonnie Gowan, Minnie Hogan, Ida Johnson, Ruby Johnson, Richadeen Lewis, Velerie Louks, Patricia O'Neil, Carol Reed, LeaAnn Smith, Annette Tracy, Karen Tyler, Patricia Vines, Della Walters, and Minnie Whitehurst.